A Pleasant ESCAPE

Praise for the author and his work

"...is like the *Five Point Someone* of IAS Aspirants. Interesting mix of fact and fiction. Youthful narrative! A fast-paced suspense: Terrific read!"

– Rohan Jha, IAS

"...brilliantly woven various motifs of the CSE journey of countless aspirants.... reflect on subtler and more important aspects of life."

– Munish Sharma, IAS (AIR 2, CSE 2013)

"One of the best contemporary youthful suspense novels I have come across."

– Hemant Rohilla, Deputy Commissioner,
Indian Revenue Service (Customs and Indirect Taxes)

"...an interesting, quick read... aspirants preparing for various competitive exams will surely identify themselves with the protagonist. A treat for suspense lovers!"

– Rohit Sahare, Assistant Commandant,
Central Industrial Security Force

"...an inimitable piece of work... witty, situational, suspenseful... a unique witty thriller!"

– Pranjal Hazarika, Joint Resident Commissioner,
UT of Daman and Diu and Dadra Nagar Haveli.

"...adventure filled novel... recommend to all suspense lovers and also to those who have, are and will be preparing for the IAS exam.'

Dr Nitin Shakya,
Assistant Collector / Sub-Divisional
Magistrate (Officer Trainee) DANICS.

"...has the right amount of drama, romance and suspense with dollops of reality. Highly recommend."

– Manish Tripathi,
Fashion Designer and Social Entrepreneur

A Pleasant ESCAPE

Piyush Rohankar

Srishti
Publishers & Distributors

Srishti Publishers & Distributors
A unit of AJR Publishing LLP
212A, Peacock Lane
Shahpur Jat, New Delhi – 110 049
editorial@srishtipublishers.com

First published by
Srishti Publishers & Distributors in 2020

10 9 8 7 6 5 4 3 2

The poems on pp 76-77, 180-181 were first published in the collection titled *Saint Hazel: Poems to a maiden,* published by Partridge in 2013. Reproduced here with requisite permissions.

Cover images sourced from Shutterstock.

Printed and bound in India

Foreword

Famous essayist Anaïs Nin was on point when she said: "We write to taste life twice, in the moment and in retrospect." With *A Pleasant Escape*, Bureaucrat Piyush Rohankar has returned to his salad days, albeit fictionally. And with each chapter, you can't help but give in completely into the main protagonist's life. I'm completely alien to the world of IAS Aspirants; the protagonist also belongs to this category. I deal with reel and here, everything is real. My profession demands me to be in the centre of showbiz, surrounded by glamour, creativity and gloss. However, in the book, the protagonist Alok's life and journey is just the opposite. So why did I instantly get drawn to it? Why did I start seeing things through his eyes? Why did I start relating to his experiences? Well, maybe because it's a tale of dreams and aspirations of young hopefuls and hence the universality of the sentiments gets to you. Piyush has woven an insightful and interesting story around the lives of UPSC examination aspirants. Personal wishes vs parental expectations, the severe pokes of heartbreak, conforming to societal norms, the constant need for validation… the youth of this country would surely see their lives reflected here.

The first-person narrative does the trick actually. I thoroughly enjoyed Alok's first tryst in Old Rajinder Nagar. The interaction with his new friend, the philosophical state of mind while smoking a cigarette alone in the balcony, the uncertainty of the future… I relived some of my own salad days with Alok. The writer has done full justice in defining each of his characters. Whether it's Alok, Gaurav, Sakshi or Ankit, you know their complete arc and yet get surprised with some of the actions. The story offers many unexpected twists and turns, which makes this book unputdownable.

What makes Piyush's writing even more compelling is his way of looking at life. Romanticising the most colourless experiences of life is an art and our author is definitely an artist. As you read the book, you would appreciate the analogies drawn by the protagonist. The comparison of an office job with an arranged marriage or a cage being disguised as a shelter... These things remain with you even after the book is done. You can see each of Piyush's joys and heartaches turned into words.

Piyush had authored three books of poetry earlier and the reading experience gets richer with the poems that are an integral part of different subplots in this book. The pace of the book will keep you engrossed. And be ready for the surprises. Happy reading!

Rahul Gangwani
Digital Editor
Filmfare

Acknowledgment

I would like to express my deepest appreciation to my father Arun Rohankar, my mother Kalpana Rohankar, my sister Akshara Rohankar and my wife Shanchui Rohankar for all the love, support and blessings they have showered upon me all through my life.

My sincere gratitude to Mr Rahul Gangwani for finding my novel worthy of his endorsement.

Special thanks to Ms Abha Iyengar and Ms Monica Dagny for the invaluable editorial assistance and for patiently helping me to explore and fine-tune the various elements related to the book.

Arup Bose, Stuti and team Srishti: Much obliged to you all for making this whole journey, of moulding my manuscript into the final product, *A Pleasant Escape!* Thank you for having faith in my work and for giving me this wonderful opportunity to reach out to the readers through your esteemed publishing house.

To all my friends and admirers of my work, thank you all for the much-needed motivation and love that you have always showered on me.

Happy reading!

Acknowledgment

Preface

Writing is like purgation of the mind, and weaving a story concatenating the beads of reality with fancy can be truly liberating. A simple white page becomes the canvas that brings to life people who leave an imprint on our minds. Sketching people and places on paper and bringing them to life in the world of the reader gave birth to the writer in me. This book has become the canvas that let me create a work of art. But in the end, it is the reader who adds true meaning to the work and who is reflected in the work. Oscar Wilde has rightly said, 'It is the spectator, and not life, that art really mirrors.'

Preparing for the toughest exam in the country not only broadened the horizons of my mind, but also honed my skills of imagination and writing to bring alive some interesting and dynamic characters and give a kaleidoscopic view of life. I intend to give a slice of the struggles faced by the aspirants who flock the mundane streets of Old Rajinder Nagar to find a gleaming future. The place becomes the microcosm of the competitive and compelling world of the aspirants. There were not many stories out there that spoke of the zeitgeist of the trying times, so I felt the need to depict a gist of it in my story.

Writing this piece of fiction has been an evolving experience for me. From where I began with my protagonist, through growing with him in his trials and tribulations, to exploring life through his eyes – it has been enriching. Hoping to find the readers enthralled as the story advances and opens a plethora of topics to ruminate on.

Piyush Arun Rohankar, DANICS.
Sub-Divisional Magistrate, Delhi Cantt.
New Delhi District

1

The Interview

"Bravo!" said Mrs Mallika Aarohi. "You really have a talent for creating fiction. The story you just narrated would make a great book."

Mrs Mallika Aarohi was an ex-IAS officer and the head of the interview panel. She and other four panel members looked quite amused. Except one gentleman, who stared intently at me.

"Thank you for your encouragement, ma'am," I said quietly. She wouldn't have believed me had I told her that the story was true.

I didn't say a word, though. I didn't want her to judge me and throw me out of the interview. It had taken me four years of spirit-destroying effort to be sitting before this panel. I wasn't going to throw it away. I did what was expected of me; I smiled politely and pretended to be gratified.

"Let's talk about people's mindset. Right and wrong depends on a person's perspective. In itself, nothing is ever right or wrong. What do you want to say about that?" Mrs Aarohi asked next.

"Madam, I would like to quote the great Turkish Sufi poet Jalal Ud-Din Muhammad Rumi here. He said, 'Out beyond ideas of right doing or wrong doing there is a field/ I will meet you there/ And when the soul lies in that field/ The world is too full to talk about…'

"A person can be judgmental or non-judgmental. Rumi urged us to be curious, but not judgmental. Only to a judgmental mind are things right and wrong." I had their rapt attention, so I continued, "I'd like to give an example. Prostitution is legalized in the West, but not in India..." Before I could complete, she pounced on me.

"What are you saying? We should legalize prostitution?" she sounded incredulous.

"I think we should sensitize people about the repercussions of not legalizing it and legalize it in the near future. We should look beyond morality and ethics because sex is a biological need. Prostitution is the oldest profession in the world. If we cannot end an evil, we should regulate it," I said, trying to look mild and harmless. It was as effective as trying to protect myself from a bullet with a sheet of newspaper. It didn't work.

"How can you say that? Don't you think we must ensure zero prostitution and rehabilitate the sex-workers?" she sounded peeved. *Damn! Why did I have to pick this example! I should have talked of doing away with jails someday in the future. That might have worked.*

The male members on the panel were silent. Some glared at me, visibly embarrassed and the rest pretended they weren't in the room. *Mature, very mature!*

I said, "Madam, we should rehabilitate the ones who want to come out of it. For those who wish to work, we must provide medical insurance and tax them." I fell silent. There was so much more to say, but my words sounded stilted even to me.

"Tomorrow you will ask to legalize murder, because that's the biological need of psychopaths," she said.

"Madam, murder is not a biological need!" I protested.

"I am talking about psychopaths!" she sounded agitated. "Isn't murder a biological need for psychopaths?"

I was petrified now, though I tried my best to look calm and harmless. Psychopaths and murder, sex and prostitution – there was no similarity!

A long silence in the midst of a discussion is considered as an acceptance of defeat. By that unspoken rule, I had lost.

"Psychopaths should be arrested and put behind bars and also treated..." I began lamely.

Before I could continue, in a firm voice she said, "Okay. Your interview is over!"

As I thanked the members of the panel, the men looked at me pityingly. They probably wondered what I was high on to speak so casually about a sensitive topic like prostitution. Well, I couldn't blame them. Just before the interview, I downed a shot of vodka to calm my nerves.

But what happened inside was destiny.

Once outside, I heaved a sigh of relief. I was sure the interview had gone on for an hour. I wished the next candidate good luck and was about to go when I heard a male voice calling my name.

It was the panel member who hadn't been amused by my story. *Did I forget anything inside? According to interview rules, you were not supposed to carry even a pen or a watch. What did he want?*

"Son, I am ex-IPS officer Rudrapratap Singh Chauhan. The girl you mentioned in your story... everything you said about her... every personal detail... matched my daughter's. Did you really know her?" he said, looking upset and anxious.

This is Sakshi's father! A shiver ran down my spine. The last time I had heard her voice was two months ago on my mobile phone, begging me to help her boyfriend and my close friend, Ankit Gupta!

And here was her father, in the flesh!

Phase 1: Preparation

2

Old Rajinder Nagar

2010, 31 May or 1 June – don't remember which, and don't care either. All you remember is that you were at the block when the race began.

Delhi was a crucible carelessly forgotten on the burner. What I had heard of Delhi heat was a pale shadow of its true horror.

Just the day before, I had bid farewell to my village, my routine and my girl – though not in that order. The other changes were inevitable, but the abrupt termination of the relationship left a nasty taste in my mouth. It was eating away at my conscience.

▼

Old Rajinder Nagar (ORN) was running on incomes from those aspiring to join government administrative services. The majority were UPSC civil service aspirants, or as they liked to call themselves, IAS aspirants – just like me.

The small shops and hotels, the unkempt restaurants, the endless coaching classes in every nook and corner were suffocating. The streets were filled with an endless supply of aspirants who were willing to let their precious youth drip away in the muggy heat to nourish the dreams of a spectacular tomorrow. The pathos of it was mind-numbing!

The rooms were crammed and barely adequate, but *home* to many like me. At first look, I wondered if I would last a week. However, I knew I would get used to the squalor. Love is not an overnight affair in an arranged marriage. It takes time. God knows this one was arranged. By parents, naturally. Who else?

Never in my life had I experienced such loneliness in a crowd. I was exhausted after my long and weary travel, and the memories of the girl now crushed under my IAS dream.

I bargained hard with the emotionless landlords and intermediaries. They knew, no matter how high a price they quoted, some aspirant or the other would readily move into the prison cell they called a *shelter*. I roamed countless lanes that had the same sorry feel about them. I finalized a room near Aggarwal Sweets in the end.

Rooms in the ORN lanes are identical. If you have money, you can afford a better one, but it hardly matters. Clearing the Civil Service exam, supposedly the toughest in the country, is a game of probability you play with a loaded dice. No matter which room you make a home in, the hopeless helplessness is the exact same in them all.

I acquired this wisdom in retrospect, of course. Most aspirants can overcome this feeling to some extent during the initial days in ORN. As the number of attempts for the UPSC exam start going up, most begin to believe in destiny rather than carving their own path.

By the time I had my new room cleaned up, the Delhi heat had rendered me half-dead. My room had an attached toilet/bathroom which I would share with the occupant of the adjoining room, currently vacant.

I had just begun unpacking my luggage when I heard a knock. It was a well-built, six-foot-tall, dark-skinned guy wearing grey-checked boxers and a black jersey. The smile on his face disappeared behind the smoke he exhaled from his mouth and nose.

That smoke smelled familiar. *Wasn't that Classic Mild?* He appeared to be a year or two older than me.

"Hey, I am Gaurav! I am a doctor... staying right opposite your door... preparing for MD...." he introduced himself, the sentence being broken down and completed after a drag or two of the cigarette.

After I introduced myself, we sat together in his room, sipping Old Monk, sharing cigarettes and stories. I called Old Monk 'students' drink' because it is the cheapest good quality liquor a student can afford.

"What made you go for Civil Services, after a degree in Engineering and Management? Didn't you get a job through campus placement?" asked Gaurav.

With a shy smile on my face, I took a drag, stalling. "Satisfaction, Gaurav. I am here for satisfaction... and a bit of respect."

After a couple of drinks both Gaurav and I were buzzed enough to let our hair down. He had his own story about how he ended up in ORN. Gaurav belonged to a bureaucratic family. His father was second in line to head the Agriculture Department in Jharkhand. He did his MBBS from a college in Pune which catered to super-rich kids. People with money are well-connected. He really didn't need to be slogging it out in ORN. He could have easily bagged a management seat in some fancy institute. His situation was as confusing to me as mine was to him.

"Why exactly did you choose to become a doctor? There is so much to study!" I said, looking around his room filled with worn-out, thick medical books. "And you don't look like the studious type, though I might be wrong. Why here, bro?" I swirled my drink, giving him time to reply.

"I wasn't bad at mathematics and physics, but I did better at biology. My physics and maths scores were less, so I concluded I was meant for medicine and not engineering," he said.

After a bit of hesitation, he added, "I wanted to go to Australia after 12th to study medicine. My score in English was the best across the country in CBSE and everything else was in place. But my parents refused to let me go to Australia; I am their only child.

"Now, five years later, they feel guilty about it, especially my dad. So here I am. I took a year off after 12th to prepare for MBBS, couldn't clear it. So my father bought me a seat in Pune. But now I want to prove my worth by fighting it out for the MD seat."

Gaurav's earnestness was amusing and impressive. Such determination is publicly displayed only after a person is slightly drunk.

After the first night of our mildly drunk interaction, I concluded that we were both equally confused about our aim in life.

▼

I woke up at 3:55 a.m., five minutes before the alarm rang. I pushed myself out of bed. Yesterday was one of the most tiring days of my life. Yet, I managed to wake up early. Such is the motivation provided by the illusion that life has a purpose. I put my excuse on a pedestal and turned it into that purpose. I was convinced that all my actions from now on would lead me to where my father thought I would have a *meaningful* life. Jogging shoes laced and headphones plugged, I left my room on the second floor in search of the garden that Gaurav had told me about. This garden was to serve as my jogging strip and workout place.

▼

It was my first day at the Khan Study Group (KSG) Civil Service coaching classes and I reached well before time. I took the tobacco-stained narrow staircase and entered the classroom on the second floor, only to find it empty.

Slowly the class began to fill up. By the time the teacher entered, there were close to a hundred students there. I was nervous, to say the least.

Twenty minutes ago, when the class was half-empty, I was high on motivation. *What had happened to my motivation now? Did I have it in me to beat the six lakh aspirants who appear for this exam, leave alone these hundred students…and make it into Civil Service?*

My mental censors couldn't stop such questions from entering my mind. To reassure myself, I tried to think about my degrees and my other talents, which I thought made me different from the crowd.

I tried face-reading people. I also observed their clothes, their mobile phones, and everything else that I could be judgmental about. It was an intimidating crowd. But then I felt someone tap my shoulder. I turned, but the voice saying, "Excuse me," reached my ears first. To my utter surprise, a beautiful girl was speaking to me. She wanted to borrow a pen.

Students stood up to greet Professor Khan, a bespectacled, fair, slightly bald man. He entered the room with a smile. His entry ensured that no further interaction took place between the two of us. So, without eye contact, I handed her my spare pen.

The first day was more like an introduction - what the exam is and how we should prepare for it in the professor's view. I paid attention and made an extra effort to control my wandering mind. When the class was over almost three hours later, everyone stood up to leave. The crowd began to look intimidating again.

I expected another tap on the shoulder, but it never came. She had been sitting right behind me, but she was gone. Had she left early? The boy who had been sitting next to her looked at me and smiled. I smiled back, but didn't enquire about the girl. I thought I would catch up with her tomorrow.

Would she remember borrowing the pen from me or would she have forgotten about the pen, about me...

I had to rush for the Psychology class, one of the two subjects I had opted for in Civil Services, the other being Philosophy.

▼

It was 2 p.m. and I was tired. I had been up since 4 a.m. I had just reached home to find a polythene bag hanging on my door along with a plastic plate. A similar polythene bag along with a plate was hanging on the opposite door also. It was my lunch.

I remembered I had asked Gaurav to start my tiffin service. The sight of food perked up my hunger. I unpacked my lunch and finished it quickly. Then I lit a cigarette and walked out to the balcony. On the opposite building's balcony, barely twelve feet away, I saw an old man with a shrivelled body, lost in thought. There was something about his gaze that told me he was ruminating on the years long gone.

I was lost in a smoke of would-bes and he was lost in a smoke of had-beens. Life does come full circle, doesn't it?

I caught up on my sleep for an hour and then went out for a cup of chai at a *tapri* (a makeshift tea-stall) across the street. I was groggy with sleep, but after a few drags from my half-burnt cigarette and a few sips of chai, I felt refreshed.

On returning to my room, I met Gaurav at his door. "Hey, dude! What's up?" I asked as Gaurav went into the common kitchen.

"Trying to stay awake, making black coffee. Would you like to have some?" he asked.

"Nah, just had chai bro. Thanks," I said and went to my room to study the hand-outs given by the General Studies professor. An objective test was scheduled for next morning and I saw it as a challenge.

I went through the hand-outs twice, and then jotted down important points in a notebook for revision for the main exams. The first round, or the prelims, were in June the next year. During the course of my preparation, I made notes for Politics Geography, History, Science and Technology, Biology, International Affairs, Environment, Psychology, Philosophy and one for Current Affairs too. I read one newspaper, *The Hindu*, and three magazines: *Yojana, Kurukshetra* and *Chronicle* religiously.

I was meticulous in my approach. I filed the hand-outs and made short notes in notebooks. I also bought geographical and political maps of India and the world, and hung them on the walls. The room no longer felt lonely.

3

Her Soon-to-be Boyfriend

The 'Pen-girl' hadn't returned my pen. I saw her in class every day, but did not approach her, though we exchanged obligatory smiles. She seemed to be a loner. I never saw her talking to anyone, and wondered, 'Are these students so dedicated to their preparation that they don't have time to talk to such a beauty in a class full of brains?'

One day in class, while I was trying to spot the Pen-girl, I saw a bespectacled boy enter late and quietly sit on the last bench. The last two rows were empty and he was sitting all alone. I had never noticed him in class before. I assumed he wasn't really serious about the exam, though his appearance belied it.

His face seemed like that of a man on a mission. His hair was unkempt and there was a look of a tuned-out scientist in his demeanour. It was as if he did not have time to notice the world because his eyes were fixed on a private inner vision.

As I came down the stairs after class, I saw Pen-girl and Mr Late talking animatedly. A wave of jealousy erupted over me. 'Why are you talking to someone who comes late to class?' I shouted to her in my head. 'Are beautiful girls this stupid? He doesn't have a future, talk to me!'

The mobile in my pocket had been vibrating, but my senses, blurred by jealousy, had ignored it.

"Get me a packet of Classic Mild, dude. I am running low on cigarettes," Gaurav said, without even bothering to say hello.

"Yes... on my way... will get it. Anything else?"

"Hmm... get me a plate of *chhola-kulcha* too. Very hungry. Haven't had breakfast yet."

"Yes sir..." I said jokingly and hung up.

▼

The next morning, class started filling up fast, but Pen-girl and Mr Late were nowhere to be seen. The professor began teaching, but even after half an hour, they weren't there.

My mind started wandering again. What if both of them enter the class together? That would be a clear sign that both of them had become good friends or begun to like each other. I was agitated that my imaginary love story would die even before becoming a love-story.

I was clear that she was the kind of girl to woo, not just be friends with. After a few more minutes, I turned to glance at the last bench again. There he was! Sitting alone, his face tense, looking straight at the board and nowhere else. Pen-girl was still nowhere to be seen. 'I still have a chance!' I grinned happily, forgetting to wonder when he had come in.

After back to back classes all morning, I was exhausted. I usually took a nap in the afternoon so I could study till late night. I didn't want to attend the afternoon class, but I didn't have a choice. More than learning the intricacies of polity, I wanted to know whether there was a romance blooming between Mr Late and Pen-girl.

I grabbed a can of Red Bull from a nearby shop and went to class. Mentally, I felt fresh; but physically, I felt a hundred years old. In the half-full class, I saw her sitting on the opposite side. We exchanged our ritualistic smile as the class began. Mr Late came thirty minutes late and sat down at his regular place, staring intently at the board.

The class got over at 6 p.m. and I took my time going downstairs. I wanted to spy on Pen-girl and Mr Late at their usual spot, but both of them were nowhere to be seen.

Gaurav called just then, asking me to bring a packet of Classic Mild and some momos. I headed to the small shop and found Mr Late and Pen-girl sitting there. I walked towards them.

The girl looked at me and smiled immediately. She said, "Hi… Wassup?"

"Hey, I am fine. Wassup with you?"

"I am great. Join us," she said, glancing at Mr Late.

I nodded and ordered a plate of momos. They refused to have any.

"This is Ankit Gupta," said the Pen-girl, introducing Mr Late.

I nodded to him.

"Hey, here's your pen! Sorry, I took it that day and kept forgetting to return it," she said with a sweet smile.

"Oh, you remember?" I said, pretending I had forgotten. "Thanks… I am sorry I still don't know your name," I played it smart.

"Sakshi Singh Chauhan," she said, smiling.

I learned that Ankit and Sakshi were engineers, two years younger to me, and this was their first attempt at UPSC, just like me.

"So, have you both known each other from before?" I asked, the serpent writhing within me.

"No, we bumped into each other when we were buying books from Kumar Book Depot," said Ankit.

Sakshi nodded, adding, "We met after Khan sir's classes started."

So their friendship was not old. The stop at the momo outlet turned into an hour-long conversation. I could feel a connection between Ankit and Sakshi. Both of them were locals and spoke familiarly of landmarks, outlets and happening places. They had a lot in common. Both their fathers were bureaucrats. Ankit's father was an IRTS officer, and Sakshi's father was an IPS officer. Ankit was born and brought up in Delhi and Sakshi was born in Banaras, but completed her education in Delhi. She had a law degree from Delhi University.

My mobile started vibrating again, and I knew it'd be Gaurav. "Hey, I have to leave. Have to buy some stuff for my friend. See you tomorrow!" I said interrupting the conversation.

"Yeah, see you tomorrow!" Sakshi smiled and Ankit waved goodbye.

I bought a packet of cigarettes and rushed home. After knocking at the door, I remembered that I had forgotten the momos. But it was too late. He opened the door and looked eagerly for them.

"Where were you? And where the fuck are the momos?" he asked, peeved.

"Sorry, forgot the momos. It just slipped my mind. Here are your cigarettes. I have to go back to buy a notebook, so will bring momos too. Give me ten minutes!" I said thrusting the cigarettes in his hands and rushing away before he could say another word.

Passing by the momo joint again on my way to the stationery shop, I saw Sakshi and Ankit still talking to each other. They didn't notice me. When I returned to get the momos packed for Gaurav, I saw them walking away together.

4

Season of Sarah

Saturday and Sundays were no longer special. Each day felt the same. It was as if somebody had erased the names of days from my calendar.

I was in class again, listening to Prof Khan in the Economics class. Since I was a Management graduate, my Economics concepts were clearer. I could answer all random questions thrown to us by him. So, some students began admiring me while some couldn't stand me. Either way, I was getting noticed. I felt as good as the devil with all the attention I got when other students came to me for notes or to have their doubts cleared. It was during one such doubt clearing session when an aspirant sitting next to me asked, "What is the difference between nominal GDP and real GDP?"

I explained both.

"Your definition is the opposite of what the book says," she said, showing me the definition from the textbook.

I looked into the book and then looked at her. We broke into giggles. Even Khan sir had agreed with my incorrect definition and had praised me for reading *The Hindu* well!

"Sorry, I got a bit confused. Too much reading of late, I guess." I tried to sound apologetic.

"It's okay. Happens…" she replied sweetly.

During the class, the thought of Sakshi crossed my mind. I turned around to spot her, and found her sitting in the last row with Ankit. Sakshi saw me and gave me a friendly smile. Ankit continued staring at the board as if he was hypnotized. But in the next three hours, I found them smiling and whispering to each other. My attention was focused on them, instead of the lesson.

When the class got over and I stood up to leave, the girl who had queried with the question on Economics, said, "Excuse me. I was absent yesterday. I missed the Science Tech class. Do you have the notes?"

"Yes, here…" I opened my bag and handed the notebook to her.

"By the way, I am Sarah Naqvi," she said smiling.

I introduced myself and told her, "There wasn't much to write yesterday, just five pages."

"Good. So it won't take much time," she said.

"Sure, let me walk you to the Xerox shop?" I asked courteously.

She agreed. As we both walked down the stairs, I saw Ankit explaining something to Sakshi animatedly.

"Where are you from?" Sarah asked me.

"Nagpur, and you?"

"Lucknow, but we stay in Jamshedpur. My Dad works in SAIL." After a bit, she asked, "What's your educational background?"

"B.Tech in Electronics and Communication and MBA in Finance," I said, bored of repeating this to everyone. "What about you?" I asked her.

"BA from Aligarh Muslim University, MA from JNU and now I am pursuing MPhil in Economics from JNU itself. After that, I plan to do my Ph.D."

Sarah wasn't explicitly beautiful like Sakshi, but she was cute. About five-feet-three, she was light-skinned and had a clear, peachy complexion. Dark, almost black eyes matched her black shoulder-length wavy hair. An assertive and outgoing girl, she was confident in the way she talked. Maybe it was the JNU effect, where they like teaching you to think and agitate – but sometimes only for the heck of agitating!

Soon, Sarah and I started sitting together in class. Her ability to discuss and debate on any random subject would blow my mind at times. *Such a clear grip on ideas and concepts! And the grit to match. There was much in her to fall for.*

We enjoyed each other's company and hung around after classes for chai and snacks. One day we both decided to bunk the Science Tech class and she came to my room to study.

We were engrossed in our own reading when she said, "I'm feeling sleepy. I'll take a nap."

I nodded and lay down on the bed too. She turned to face me and started playing with my ear. My heart started thumping. The next moment, we were kissing. But soon, we left to attend the second half of the class we had bunked, knowing well that we wouldn't be able to study in my room anymore.

On the way to the class in a rickshaw, Sarah asked, "Do you think our relationship would work? My parents won't allow me to marry a Hindu."

I shook my head as we made our way into the class. And as usual, Ankit and Sakshi sat together.

▼

UPSC Civil Service is a three-tier exam. Post-2011, in the new system, Paper-I was General Studies and Paper-II was Common Aptitude test (CSAT), compulsory for everyone. Since it had compulsory sections on English and maths, students from various backgrounds were nervous about it.

"*Ya Allah,* these UPSC mother-fuckers had to go and change the syllabus right now, when I am taking the exam," grunted Mustafa.

Mustafa was from Kargil and knew Gaurav from school days. Mustafa was a tall guy. He looked handsome with his curly brown hair, fair skin and startling green eyes. He had a Grecian cast to his face. It was finely chiselled face like that of a Michelangelo sculpture.

It was Mustafa's second attempt at the Civil Services exam. This year, with maths, logic and reasoning being part of CSAT, he thought it had become even more difficult for him since he was a law graduate and maths wasn't his forte.

As we sat discussing CSAT in Gaurav's room, Sarah called up on my cell phone, saying she was planning to stay with me that night. Our relationship was almost four months old but this was a first.

She had brought with her a coil heater as December is quite bone-chilling in Delhi. It wasn't easy to focus on modern Indian history while Sarah sat next to me, cosily wrapped up in the same *rajai*. Thankfully, she put away her MPhil work and turned to me. We began kissing and another study session turned into a kissing and petting session. She refused to go all the way, though.

"There is still time for all that," she said.

As desperate as I was to experience love at its fullest, consent was also important. The morning found us both wrapped in each other and the rajai.

It was the first time I had slept with a girl in my arms the whole night. It was a heady feeling. It was 7 a.m. and bitterly cold. She was still sleeping, so I went to make some tea for her.

When tea was ready, I kissed her sweet morning mouth to wake her up. "What would you like for breakfast?" I asked her.

"Anything," she mumbled, half-asleep.

She had classes that day and JNU was a long way from Karol Bagh. She left after having chai, Maggi, and a few more kisses, hugs and I love yous from me.

5

Virginity Woes

The test series were now about to begin. I was done with my classes and needed to revise General Studies as much as possible before the Prelims.

The vast syllabus couldn't be memorized. Prof Khan and many other veterans of Civil Service preparation advised that all you could do was to read everything over and over again so that you could eliminate options on the answer sheet instinctively and increase the probability of ticking the right option. I intended to follow this advice to the 'T'.

During our coaching classes at Khan Study Group, Sakshi, Ankit and I decided to exchange weekly notes of *The Hindu, Economic Times, Indian Express* and any other subject concerning current affairs. In the past four-five months, we had met regularly to exchange notes at a deserted Café Coffee Day (CCD) outlet on the first floor of the building next to Karol Bagh metro station. This CCD had become our meeting point.

Sakshi and Ankit were in love. I could see it on their faces although they pretended that they were just friends.

"I can barely devote six to seven hours a day for UPSC. Have to study for my law exams too. God save me. What about you?" Sakshi asked looking at me.

"Going good. Ten to eleven hours a day," I replied. "What about you Ankit?"

"Even I am not able to study as much as I ought to if I want to clear this exam," replied Ankit.

"That doesn't answer my question," I said politely.

"Hmm, maybe twelve," said Ankit after giving a thought.

"That's good, Ankit. Why did you say, not much?"

"Because I've heard that those who clear Civil Services exam study for eighteen hours a day consistently. At times the fear of failure paralyzes me and ruins my concentration. I just can't focus then," he said. His frown had deepened. Sakshi winked at him and patted his back.

I smiled thinking – 'He's clocking thirteen hours a day or more, yet he laments that he isn't giving his best! I bet his concentration is ruined by the thoughts of his gorgeous girlfriend, not fear of failure!'

Honestly, I couldn't study either when Sarah came down. We would sit down with our books and pretend to study. It would invariably end in a kissing session by the end of which we'd be too tired to focus on anything exam related.

The date for the Prelims was out. It was going to be held on 12 June and it was already 1 March. We still had three months to revise whatever we had studied in the past nine months. We were enthusiastic and excited.

On my way back home, I met Abhijeet and Rohini, both IAS aspirants in one of the coaching classes. Abhijeet was as serious an aspirant as Ankit, but one who reached class thirty minutes early to grab a front row seat, like me.

Abhijeet was a tall and handsome Jat from Rajasthan. His voice had a natural authority to match his commanding personality. Under the thick mass of his hair, his dark eyes bore into you with mesmerizing intensity.

Rohini was thin, tall, bespectacled and sported a braided ponytail. Until she spoke, she looked like a mousy, quiet girl who wouldn't say boo to a docile cat. But that impression was completely the opposite of truth.

She matched his ferociousness of manner. They were like deadly assassins on a mission to kill the exam! They asked questions aggressively, each fed by the energy of the other. *They must be dynamite in bed!*

As this thought crossed my mind, I remembered that Sarah would be coming for another night stay! I grinned. *Will today be the day I'll get lucky?*

I cleared up the soiled underwear and crumpled newspapers lying around in the room. I sprayed my deodorant since I had no room-freshener. At least, the place should smell good.

I picked Sarah up and we fell upon each other as soon as we entered the room. We were going at it hot and hard when her phone rang. It was her mother and she had to take it. She received the call and went out into the balcony.

The call went on for some twenty odd minutes and when the call got over, I took her in my arms and tried to resume. But she pulled away and said we should eat first.

I ordered biryani from a food-joint nearby. After the meal, we lay down to watch a movie.

"Are you crying!? Why? What happened? Are you alright?" I asked, shocked.

"My parents want me to get married. They have arranged for me to meet a guy," she said.

"Who guy?" I asked. I felt as if a block of ice slid down my gullet and landed in my gut.

"He is the son of the Chief Secretary of Uttar Pradesh," she said through stiff lips.

"So, will you meet him?" I asked, forcing the words out.

"I don't want to," she said breaking into a fresh barrage of tears. "I don't know what to do!"

"Can't you postpone this for a year? I'll have cleared the UPSC or I'll get some other job," I said, my heart pounding. *Why the hell don't parents leave us alone! What's the hurry with getting married? This is stupid!*

"I love you, but I don't know what to do…" She sobbed, hiding her face in my chest, her arms clinging to me desperately.

I kissed her wet cheeks and gathered her closer to me. "We will find a way out, don't worry." I consoled her.

"There is no way out. I don't know what to do, but I love you so much," she wailed.

My eyes filled up too and an involuntary sob broke out from me. She kissed me fiercely, her tongue invading my mouth with the right of ownership. Almost in a trance, we helped each other out of our clothes.

"I want you tonight," she said simply. "Do you?"

I nodded, too overcome to speak.

I couldn't do it. It was extremely painful. I was afraid I would tear my foreskin and start to bleed. We had to give up the idea of having sex just yet. I don't know which one of us was more disappointed.

The next morning, Sarah left without giving me any assurances. Instead, she asked me to take our relationship one day at a time, leaving me utterly despondent.

To get my mind off the bleakness of it all, I spent the day on the internet, in research. Apparently, my foreskin had got stuck at the tip and couldn't slide back. I needed to consult a doctor.

Gaurav! The thought of him was too embarrassing. What if he teased me, or told Mustafa? I called up a doctor friend who had been my junior in school. He told me that he had had a similar problem and the cure for it was a minor operation. The operation involved a slight removal of foreskin from the tip to ease the sliding of the skin.

Was he talking of circumcision? I did plan to convert to Islam to marry Sarah, but I didn't want to get circumcised right now. It would be so painful.

6

Almost Caught at JNU

The uncertainty about my relationship with Sarah had plunged me in an overwhelming misery and confusion. I was thinking about it constantly. My focus had gone for a toss.

I bumped into Ankit when returning from one of the test centres. He was alone. Earlier we had decided to stop the exchange of weekly notes because of our conflicting schedules.

"How are you, bhai? How is your Prelims prep going?" I asked.

"Not doing much, yaar. I haven't started full-fledged yet," said Ankit, blinking sleepily.

"Joined any Prelims test series?"

"I'll give it at KSG. but will focus on Prelims after 15 April. Until then, I will try to finish revising my optional subject."

"That sounds like a good idea," I said. "How is Sakshi? Do you guys hang around much?"

"Rarely. She is busy with her University law exams. She wanted to meet today, but I declined. I know she has been finding it difficult to balance her college, UPSC studies and us meeting. But we do talk on telephone every day for at least an hour," he said, his ears turning pink.

I was happy that Sarah and I met at my room every Saturday and Sunday, although she did complain that I never paid her a visit at JNU.

▼

The next time she brought up the topic, I tried to explain to her the benefit of meeting in my room. It gave us the privacy we needed, which wouldn't be possible at JNU.

"Oh, so we meet only to make out?" her brow had furrowed.

"No, but we meet after a considerable gap and then it is obvious that we do feel like making out," I said. Even to me, the words sounded lame.

"I know, but I would feel better if you come to my college. My other friends' boyfriends come to meet them. The campus is vast, with many eateries which serve delicious food!" she coaxed.

A long silence followed after this and then again she said, "Next time I want you to come and meet me at campus, or else I will never come to your room!" She turned her face away. It wasn't an empty threat; I knew she meant it.

▼

I decided to visit her at JNU. On the way, I got her some chocolates. Along with chocolates, I was also carrying the poem I had composed for her. I reached the JNU campus around 5 p.m. She took me to Parthasarthi Rock on her scooty, named after a former JNU chancellor. It was the highest point in JNU. We sat there for some time talking to each other. After giving the chocolates to her, I rolled out the poem.

"I wrote something for you, Sarah," I said.

"What?"

"It is a poem. Um... just something I scribbled," I said, staring down at the piece of paper.

"When did you start writing?"

I just made a face trying to remember exactly when I wrote my first poem. "Doesn't matter," she continued, seeing that I was not going to reply to that question, "Will you read it out for me?"

To Love Her Is Like a Journey

And to love her is like a journey,
Not a casual stroll or an adventure,
But a patient walk of a million miles,
And slowly her myth unfolds,
As she reveals herself in layers,
Her beauty has all the shades of life,
But I fall short of colours to paint her glory,
Oh, to love her is like a journey,
A journey of a million miles....

And I am still exploring,
the darkest corners of her soul,
Of what lay beneath those eyes,
And I am still exploring,
The mysticism she practices with her smile,
Her incandescent calligraphic elegance,
Her magnetism has pulled me in her labyrinthine life,
I still walk those virgin Forrest she drew for me,
Where the words that kissed her lips,
Still echoes like an infectious melody,
Oh her beauty and my youth,
Had led me into believing that life would go on forever,
Oh to love her is like a journey,
A journey of a million miles....

And all the falling stars that I saw as a child,
I found them at her feet,
And my joy to watch her dance,
over them in her Carmel,
She is the romance of a winter love story,

The picture of a million memories,
The blood of God flows through her heart,
The space in between her arms,
Is the doorway to heaven,
the light for my mornings comes from her smile,
Oh, to love her is like a journey,
A journey of a million miles…."

The moment I finished reading my poem, she grabbed me by the collar and kissed me. I wanted the kiss to continue, but I wasn't comfortable kissing in public.

"Thanks for coming," she said. "Isn't JNU a beautiful place?"

"It is indeed, my love, but a bit far from my place. I really wanted to meet you."

"Ooooh, really?" she asked, a mischievous smile on her face. "You really wanted to meet me or was it because I threatened you?"

"You figured it out!" I laughed. "That is the reason I came running! The main reason for me not to come down to JNU is that I am actually feeling the exam pressure. There is way too much to study."

"I can understand, baby! I have to find time for my MPhil, Civil Service studies as well as our relationship. You don't have any burden other than Civil Service studies. You will have to manage, darling," she said, holding my hand. "Oh, there is some good news! The guy my parents arranged for me to meet with, remember? His marriage has been fixed somewhere else, suddenly. The girl he is marrying, her family made an offer which they could not refuse," she finished in a thick voice, Marlon Brando style.

I flung my arms around her and crushed her to me, kissing her fiercely, possessively. *Thank you, god!* Excitedly, we talked of better days to come as the soothing evening enveloped us in its velvet arms.

We went out for a walk. She took my hand and pulled me into an isolated power-generation room. We ducked behind it and started making out. Just after a couple of minutes or so, however, we heard footsteps and voices.

From the trees that covered the isolated power generation room, we could see some students approaching. They were busy chatting with each other, discussing a football game from which they were returning. They didn't expect anyone to be there. Thankfully the evening dusk saved us. Had it been daytime, we would surely have been caught because we were easily visible through the trees as the room was at an elevation, and the path below it was used by students as a shortcut to the playgrounds. We waited for the sound of their footsteps to subside.

"We must leave," Sarah said, her voice low.

I protested, "They have left, let's continue."

"No! We might get caught. As it is the mood on the campus about such going-ons is pretty volatile because of a recent incident," she said.

"Which incident?"

"An MMS is doing the rounds on the campus. It's about two hostellers. The guy recorded a sex session between him and his girlfriend. Then he tried to blackmail her into marrying him because she was getting married to someone else. The video got leaked and both of them have got suspended. Now the campus is rife with moral policing. I don't want to get suspended," she declared.

She saw my crestfallen face and smiled naughtily. "Don't worry, I will pay you a visit soon, darling!"

7

Our New Neighbour

Somewhere in the second week of March 2011, when I returned after giving one of the mock Prelims test paper, I saw someone sitting in Gaurav's room, his luggage scattered in the room next to Gaurav's.

"Hey, dude! This is Manish Pandey, our new neighbour," said Gaurav introducing us.

We shook hands. His grip was firm and intimidating; the backs of his hands hairy. Manish was short and slim. He wore thick, rectangular-framed glasses, giving him a small-town boy air. I wasn't wrong. He was from Samasthipur, Bihar. A melancholic smile with a strange monotonous way of talking proclaimed him an oddball.

The three of us sat in Gaurav's room for an hour discussing our studies. Gaurav and I told Manish about the entrance exams both of us were preparing for and the fun we had pulling each other's leg on the probability we had of clearing them, given the sporadic effort. We briefed Manish about the different coaching classes, the tiffin service, the maid and other things one should know to make life a little comfortable in Old Rajinder Nagar.

Over time, Manish's simplicity was apparent. His habits, the way he thought and spoke were straightforward. He gave himself no airs. I believe, unlike others, his reasons for trying for the civil services were pure, though he never explicitly told us why he wanted to become a civil servant.

"When the time is right, I tell you why I want to become a civil servant. Until then I will dedicate all my energies to clearing the exam so that I can serve the country and help bring justice to those who need it the most." His words hinted at a tragic past.

Manish idolized Gandhi. He wanted to curb corruption and work for the masses. He was a be-a-part-of-the-solution-and-not-the-problem kind of guy. He was a farmer's son. When we talked about farmer suicides in Vidharbha, he got agitated and emotional.

"You carry this diary with you everywhere. I've seen you note things in it all the time. What do you write in it?" I asked him one day.

"This is my blueprint diary," he said mysteriously.

"Blueprint for what?" I asked, bristling with curiosity.

"Blueprint for a better India. I note down ideas I will implement when I become a civil servant," he said simply.

In spite of myself, I was impressed. He had said *when* not *if.* It wasn't an empty boast. He *knew* what he wanted to do with his life in a compelling, non-negotiable way.

"Hey, may I take a peek into your diary and steal a few ideas?" I teased.

"Someday I will publish my diaries under the title *My Existential Struggle*. You can read it then." He grinned.

Gaurav had taken an instant liking to Manish. He was helpful and often prepared breakfast and chai for us. Gaurav and he would talk for hours about life and studies.

Gaurav enjoyed his fame as the 'doctor to the UPSC aspirants'. The other doctors in Old Rajinder Nagar would charge five hundred bucks as consultation fees, after student discount. Many of my friends, and their friends, would consult Gaurav for free.

▼

Manish was the early-to-bed-early-to-rise type. Each morning Gaurav was woken by the sound of prayer bells as Manish prayed.

"Today Manish didn't pray, nor did he prepare chai and breakfast. Isn't he in his room?" Gaurav remarked when I strolled into his room for our morning smoke.

"Don't know, dude. He is your neighbour. You must know better."

The door to Manish's room was locked from inside and there was no response from him when we knocked.

"This is a little worrying. Just yesterday he was telling me about his high blood pressure problem. I hope he hasn't passed out!" Gaurav exclaimed.

"Why do you have to think negative all the time, bhai? He might have studied all night and is now catching up on his sleep," I said in a feeble attempt to reassure us both.

After five minutes of gentle knocking and shouting his name, we started to bang his door harder, but to no avail. We got scared.

Finally, we broke the lock and found him lying unconscious on his bed. Gaurav checked his pulse, it was faint. We immediately took him to Sir Ganga Ram Hospital and got him admitted.

The doctors said he had passed out because of high blood pressure and that he must always monitor it. Manish was discharged after a couple of days. He looked weak and frail but it did not deter him from his goal. The day after getting discharged, he got back to his rigorous routine of studies and prayers. His commitment to his dream was commendable and inspiring.

Manish's idealism burned with a brighter flame when Anna Hazare's anti-corruption crusade for Jan Lokpal burst over India in the summer of 2011. He jumped into the movement with both eager feet.

"Do you think this is a good idea?" Gaurav asked him one evening.

"I can't say until I try," said Manish. "Look, I have seen poverty from up close. I know problems are aggravated by corruption and inefficient bureaucracy. They are the root of social injustice and inequality. If the

Jan Lokpal Bill is passed, things will improve drastically. I cannot sit on my hands when a movement of this magnitude and scope is sweeping the nation. I must be a part of it, I simply must!" he declared, his voice ringing with passion.

"But you aren't fully recuperated yet!" said Gaurav.

"Don't you worry about me! I'll be absolutely fine. This movement has filled me with energy!" Manish said, clapping a hand on Gaurav's shoulder.

"Please don't go, my friend," I begged. "If you don't want to listen to me, at least listen to Gaurav, he is a doctor. The summer heat is going to suck the life out of you. Such demonstrations are not democratic. They are holding the government hostage. You want to be a Civil Servant. Don't get into all this. Recover and study for the Prelims. Hardly two months to go..." All my appeals, sane or otherwise, fell on deaf ears.

"There's nothing you or anyone else can say that would change my mind. I will rest better at the Jantar Mantar, knowing that I am contributing in creating a better future for us all. In fact, you should come and join the movement too! Let's give Annaji a chance. Come, my brothers, come with me..." He stalked out of the room with patriotic zeal, wearing his Gandhi cap.

As he was going down the stairs, Gaurav rushed out and shouted, "Do give us a call if your health worsens. We are proud of you..."

Gaurav didn't hear Manish say anything but he saw him waving his hand, looking up at him with a quiet smile on his face.

Anna's Jan Lokpal movement was gathering steam in Delhi. This movement captured the imagination of many Indians in India and across the world. The country was up in arms. News channels were tearing the government apart. Every move at Jantar Mantar was being covered. Different personalities including cricketers and actors paid visits to Jantar Mantar to pay tribute to Annaji.

Gaurav and I were also charged up. Every day we discussed the agitation and its impact on the politics of the country. There was a growing awareness amongst people about their rights. Social media was already buzzing with anti-corruption messages.

"The outcome of this demonstration and fasting at Jantar Mantar would not really be the game-changer in the fight against corruption. The ones in power would somehow still be able to fool the masses and Annaji," Gaurav predicted, having seen bureaucrats and politicians from up close.

I was optimistic though. Annaji's decision to fast until death if the Jan Lokpal Bill was not passed, electrified India across all demographics. Many fasted with Annaji. In one of the columns of *The Hindu*, we saw a photo of Manish. He was sporting the "I am Anna" cap and his eyes were closed as if he was meditating in the sun. We were proud, but concerned.

The article was titled "The Youth of the country are responding to Anna's Call". Those fasting would fast until the Jan Lokpal bill was passed. Terrified, we called Manish.

"Hey, guys! How are you?" said Manish.

"We are fine Manish, just saw a picture of you in *The Hindu*. We are proud of you, but extremely worried too. The article said the fasting will last until the government gives in. Your body isn't meant for that, you know. Please eat something!"

"Don't worry about me, my friends! Nothing will happen to me. The blessings of millions who have suffered because of corruption are with me. I am feeling fine! If my health deteriorates, I will surely call you guys. Thanks for the concern. Anna is going to address the gathering soon, I will talk to you guys later. Jai Hind!" His weak voice rang with the pride of being a part of something he believed in.

Celebrities were pouring in at Jantar Mantar. Amir Khan, Farhan Akhtar and Anupam Kher were there, pledging their support for Anna's movement, along with the Oscar-winning music director, A.R.

Rahman. But the deadlock persisted. However, as the days passed by, a glimmer of hope arose and it looked like the government might give in after all. The pressure from all strata of society was mounting. Industrialists, senior bureaucrats, technocrats and world leaders of some countries also threw their weight behind this movement by raising concerns about the seriousness of the government towards fighting corruption.

On 15 April, the Parliament decided to pass a resolution in which the House reached an understanding that the Jan Lokpal Bill would be passed. Some people were foxed by the parliament's ambiguous declaration to adopt the Jan Lokpal Bill. Nonetheless, many were celebrating.

Anna, however, decided to end his fast a day after the above declaration. Gaurav and I wanted to catch up on this much-celebrated event. We looked forward to meeting Manish at Jantar Mantar. On 16th April, as we reached Jantar Mantar, the atmosphere was electrifying. Scores of supporters were getting ready to break their hunger strike with Annaji.

According to reports, close to one hundred and fifty people were on hunger strike along with Manish. But we couldn't see him anywhere. The last time we had spoken to him, he said he would keep his phone switched off since his charger was not working properly and there were not many charging points nearby.

We started asking people at Jantar Mantar about Manish, describing him and showing his photo on Gaurav's phone. No one could identify him. After Anna Hazare broke his fast, the crowd started to disperse.

"Maybe he went back home," I said with fake excitement. Instead of voicing the worst, Gaurav too joined in and said, "Yeah, perhaps. If anything had happened to him at Jantar Mantar, it would definitely have been reported in the media. Their TRP hounds pounce upon any tragic incidents in a revolutionary cause." We left Jantar Mantar, hoping to find Manish at home. Manish didn't show up all night.

Early the next morning, Gaurav received a call from Ram Manohar Lohia hospital. He was called because the last call received on Manish's phone was from Gaurav. Manish was dead!

We rushed to the hospital. The doctor took us to the morgue. There were tears in our eyes as we looked at Manish's pale lifeless body.

"Cause of death?" asked Gaurav, trying to stifle his sobs.

"He was suffering from cancer. Cause of death was multiple organ failure. His fast had made his body weak. His blood pressure was unstable because of multiple tumours situated on the spinal cord and arteries," the doctor said in a flat, emotionless voice.

"When he was brought here, he was weak but conscious. He was muttering something about a yellow diary. If you know anything about it, please do inform his parents," the doctor finished drily.

We called Manish's father and gave him the terrible news. I found his yellow diary on his table. *Why was he muttering about the diary? Did he know he was going to die? He wanted it to be left in safe-keeping maybe?*

In the diary, very few entries were happy. It seemed Manish was mostly worried or sorrowful. His words, his thoughts, were sombre. As I read the diary, I could see why Manish was so intense.

The diary was a record of the story of a poor boy from Samasthipur, Bihar. Of how he worked in hotels and garages to save money in order to fulfil his dream of being an IAS officer. Manish's dad was a poor farmer and their family had to go through a lot of hardship caused by the double menace of drought and moneylenders. But that was not the worst of the adversities the family had to go through. There was worse.

Manish had an elder sister who was a schoolteacher. As soon as she started working, Manish's family hoped their financial troubles would soon be over. However, their hopes were short-lived.

His sister was old enough to be married. But the proposals came with a demand for hefty dowry. His father sold off half his agricultural land to arrange the dowry and made the wedding arrangements. A few months into the marriage, her in-laws started harassing her for more money. One day, Manish's sister disappeared. Her in-laws tried to make it appear as if she had run away with some man and that they had nothing to do with her disappearance.

After a few days of filing the missing person report, the decomposed body of his sister was found in a suitcase abandoned at the Patna railway station. A post-mortem showed severe burns and multiple injuries on the body. A case of murder, domestic violence and dowry was registered against her husband's family. Her in-laws bribed the police heavily. The investigation was botched up and the evidence deliberately destroyed. Her in-laws went scot-free.

Manish's family not only lost the case but were also threatened with dire consequences. Manish's father, fearing for the life of the rest of the family, which included Manish's younger sister, submitted to the pressure and didn't pursue the case any further. Manish could never forgive his sister's husband and in-laws, the society, the corrupt police, lawyers and judiciary who were all equally responsible for the death of his sister. Instead of becoming a vigilante, Manish chose the path of civil services and swore to bring such murderers and criminals to justice.

▼

That night, Gaurav and I couldn't sleep.

We sifted through every newspaper and searched online through the reports of all television channels, there was no mention of Manish's death, the only victim of Anna Hazare's Jan Lokpal hunger strike. We called up a reporter and told him about Manish's death due to fasting at the Jantar Mantar protest. The reporter promised to look into the matter. When he finally did call back, it was to tell us that he would not be able to publish this news because the death certificate cited the cause of death as cancer, and not fasting.

Times magazine later ranked the Anna Hazare movement as one of the top ten movements of the year 2011. In our mind, the movement was forever associated with the death of a quiet, idealist boy, our wonderful friend Manish.

8

Mourning amidst Tension and Sex

May in Delhi is revolting. I wanted to scrape my skin off and take up permanent residence in a pool of ice. But the heat wasn't my biggest torture. The thoughts of Manish tormented me without respite. The fact that he still retained faith in the system which had short-changed him so cruelly shook me to the core.

For Gaurav too, Manish's death was an unbearable tragedy. He took it harder than I did. For weeks we talked about Manish incessantly, it was only natural.

"Manish has made me question my choices and the motivation behind them," I said to Gaurav one evening. "He had every right to turn bitter and cynical, but he didn't. Honestly Gaurav, my reasons for going for civil services were insincere and shallow. I looked upon a civil services job as something that would give me a good life. Now, because of Manish, my outlook is completely altered. As if Manish had passed the torch of his idealism and passion to me before he bid the world goodbye! Serving the nation with sincerity and devotion will now be my passion!"

Gaurav gripped my arm, too overcome to say a word. I know what he meant though.

The Prelims were just a month away. All my debates and discussions about the Anna Hazare anti-corruption movement with other aspirants became opportunities for me to talk about Manish. I felt his life story was worth knowing and learning from. However, beyond a few words of sympathy, nobody had the time to dwell on the subject.

With all these events, I sounded despondent so often over the phone that Sarah paid me a surprise visit one morning.

I heard a knock on my door. "Come in! It's open," I yelled, expecting it to be Gaurav. Instead of the door opening, there was another knock. Irritated, I flung the door open to find Sarah standing with a sweet smile on her face.

"Hey! This is such a pleasant surprise!" I said as I hugged her close.

"Well, it's been a month since we last met. You sound so forlorn since Manish that I decided to cheer you up a little," she said and planted a quick kiss on my cheek.

Even with her, I couldn't help bringing up Manish. I could barely study for five hours a day. Gaurav hadn't been studying at all for the past fifteen days. He spent all his time watching movies and drinking.

"This world is a fucking farce," I said to Sarah. "No one cares about anyone's life. Poor Manish died for a cause and no one, not even Anna Hazare, recognizes Manish's sacrifice. He could have easily stayed home. Why did he have to go? Why?!" I wiped my tears away, but it was pointless. The dam had broken. Sarah held me close and I let the tears come.

"You should be proud of Manish," she said after a while. "How many people do you know who have the passion and courage to give up their life for a cause? You should focus on the Prelims. Manish would be really proud of you if you crack this exam and fulfil his dream of a corruption-free India!"

Unable to contain my frustration, I said, "This country deserves to be the way it is! We are the most corrupt nation in the world. We're a self-centred population of 1.2 billion people, multiplying like virus. All anyone cares about is filling their stomach.

"I wish I could have explained this to Manish, but Manish was infested with hope. It was his damned hope that killed him. Our country's woes are many. Not only do we lack economic infrastructure but social and societal inequalities have aggravated our challenges. India is a person plagued with multiple diseases. And Manish thought he could find a cure for this sick nation by sacrificing his precious life!

"Do you think people preparing for Civils have any wish to eradicate corruption? Oh, no! They jump onto the corruption bandwagon too. Look at the way people talk about the scope of making money as a civil servant! They don't care about people like Manish. They will only remember some fucked-up guy who would get lucky and become All India Rank 1!" I panted, having run out of steam.

Sarah grabbed me by my collar and kissed me hard, her tongue in my mouth. I guess that was the only way she could shut me up. Sarah and I almost ripped each other's clothes off.

"Don't! Be careful!" Sarah's moan broke my trance. Before I realized what was going on, I experienced a warm, wet release from my body. As I fell flat on Sarah breathing heavily, she hugged me tightly.

"High on emotions, high on sex, huh? I think you should always be depressed. You fuck well when you are in the grip of strong emotion. C'mon now! Be a good boy and get me an I-pill from the nearest chemist. I feel shy buying it myself," said Sarah, a pleased smile lighting up her eyes.

When I made no effort to get off the bed, she said, "You better go and get it. Do you want me to get pregnant?"

"What? We had sex?" *I lost my virginity and it wasn't painful!*

"Of course we did, you silly thing!" she said, slapping my wrist playfully.

I left the room to get the I-pill for her. At the chemist's, I ran into Ankit.

"Dude, where are you going?" I asked.

"I was searching for your place an hour ago. Finally managed to find it, but on my way up to your room, I met your neighbour. He told me you weren't there. So I returned. Where were you?"

"That's strange. An hour ago… I was in my room. Did Gaurav tell you I wasn't there?" *But Gaurav was at his friend's place since yesterday.*

"Whom did you meet?" I asked, puzzled.

"I don't recall his name. He was short and thin. Had dark circles under his eyes…"

That sounded like Manish, not Gaurav! How was that possible? Manish has been dead for fifteen days!

"It doesn't matter, forget it," said Ankit, interrupting my thought process. "What are you doing here? Not well?"

"Well, Sarah's not feeling well. Just a runny nose, nothing much. Why don't you come to my room now and we can discuss the topic? I'll introduce you to Sarah also."

"Wish I could, but I have to meet Sakshi. She has been asking me to meet her for a long time. I come to Old Rajinder Nagar often. This place is like home to me. I find myself wandering aimlessly here at times. I don't like this place, but I don't feel at ease anywhere else," said Ankit. I couldn't have agreed more with the last part of his sentence.

When I returned, Sarah was waiting for me. "What took you so long, bitch?" she said mischievously.

"I met Ankit so stopped for a chat," I said.

"Who is Ankit?" she asked, popping the pill into her mouth.

"The guy who studies with us in KSG. You know he is dating Sakshi. Hope you recall her at least!" I said.

"God only knows who you are talking about. Never met either of them in class or saw you talking to them. But it is hardly surprising. Our class is a fucking fish market! Anyway, I am starving. Order a pizza for me. And don't start crying about Manish again or else…" Before she could finish her sentence, I found myself over her, kissing her neck, smelling her hair. I just couldn't resist Sarah when she used the F-word and sounded a bit angry. I made love to Sarah for the second time that day.

9

The Unexpected Night

Days before the exam, apart from the one or two cans of Red Bull per day, the only other way I dealt with my stress was with increased consumption of cigarettes and porn. The stakes were very high. Days, where I started out as a zealous and disciplined aspirant following a healthy regime, were long gone. I now slept at 4 a.m. often instead of waking up at that hour. Fatigue had set in and morning jogs were no longer a part of my daily routine. A whole year of preparation was coming to an end. If I failed in Prelims this year, the wait till the next one would be long, painful and full of self-doubt.

One night, anxiety had got the better of me. I was all alone in the flat. Gaurav had gone to his friend's place for group studies and no new tenants had come to occupy the other two rooms.

I was already two cans down on Red Bull along with ten sticks of Classic Mild that resulted in a charged up day and very sleepless night. My stomach rumbled with hunger and I cooked Maggi on the electric heater-cum-stove that Sarah had given me. The clock read 3 a.m. and the calendar read 2nd June. *Ten more days to go*.

The air cooler hummed in the background while I went through the life of Henry Vivian Dorazio. He was a young Anglo-Indian poet from Bengal, who was considered the first freedom fighter poet. Poor Dorazio died of tuberculosis at a young age; it reminded me of Manish. I could hear him now, talking with his sincere face, his voice passionate. The noise of air cooler drowned in the boom of Manish's voice. That's when I heard a knock. *Who could it be at 4 a.m.? Must be Gaurav.* I peeped through the eyehole in the door, but couldn't see anyone's face because the stairs leading to our floor had no light.

"Who is it?" I called out, my palms suddenly clammy.

I heard a voice. It sounded as if someone was sobbing. It scared the hell out of me. I shouted again, "Who is it? What do you want?"

"Ankit!" was all I could hear. I felt a bit relieved but at the same time perplexed too. This is not how I expected Ankit's first visit to my room to be.

"Sorry. I didn't know where else to go. Couldn't think of anyone else," said Ankit, when I let him in. He sat on my bed as I latched up the door.

"What happened, dude? You look very disturbed. What brings you to my doorstep at this unearthly hour?"

"It's Sakshi. She hasn't been taking my calls. I just can't focus. I have been listening to motivational songs but it's just not working. Do you know I cleared CAT and even got into IIM Lucknow and MDI Gurgaon? But I gave it up for Civil Service. Now, because of a girl, I am not able to focus. I am in love, but she wouldn't understand that I am doing it all for her."

"Calm down, dude! Here, drink some water. Now tell me what the problem is?"

He ignored the water and said, "She wants me to spend more time with her. I told her I would, once the Prelims were over. Moreover, we do speak on the phone. But she wants to meet me every other day. Once I clear the exam, I will spend my days and nights with her for the rest of my life! But until then, she should understand that her man is trying to do his best to make a career for himself and give her the life she deserves. Why doesn't she get it?" he asked in despair as he held his head in his hands, frustrated.

"You need to relax. She must be going through a mood swing. You know how girls are! Even Sarah does all this drama. Girls have this inborn talent for the artificial creation of tension. It's 4:30 a.m. Why don't you try to just sleep on it? I'm sure things will be fine soon. If you want, I'll give her a call and try to put your point across so that she understands... hmm? I don't want to encroach on your privacy; I just want to help."

Ankit said, "I don't know, man. I know she speaks to you but generally, she is a very private person and I don't know if she would like to talk to you about our personal relationship. If it doesn't work, instead of improving the situation, it might end up making it worse. Is there any other way?"

"I write poems. You can borrow one of my poems and send it to her! What do you say?"

"Let's try, I see no harm. Hope it works because her not talking to me is making me go crazy. Please help me out with this!"

"Relax, I think I have the poem you need for this particular situation," I said.

"Here you go," I said, and handed him the poem. He read it aloud as if he was reciting it in an elocution contest.

Her Silence

"Will I find a place in your memory?
Or if you choose to write a story,
I wonder if you will remember?
Or will I be your forgotten December?
Is this your final goodbye?
These seven days of silence,
How am I supposed to read it?

Should I wait for more silence to follow,
Some more patience to swallow?
Is this your final goodbye?
How can I hear you
From the calls you don't receive?
Your words that are hard to come by
Through the letters you don't reply
Tell me how can I see you,
Through this veil of silence?
Your pictures from the past,
They refuse to speak,
They tell a different story now,
From what they did back then,
Have the sweet grapes of love turned sour?
Why this silence at this point of hour?
What words should I choose?
To break this silence that grows evermore,
Tell me, what words should I choose
To end this emotional abuse?
What went wrong in your heart
That you are falling apart?
Oh, let's go back to the start!

Will I find a place in your memory?
Or if you choose to write a story,
I wonder if you will remember
Or will I be your forgotten December?"

"Wow, this is some impressive stuff. If this doesn't work, then I don't know what will," said Ankit. "Give me a piece of paper, I'll copy it down. Thank you! You're a life-saver!"

"Sleep on my bed for a few hours, Ankit!" I offered.

"Yes, I am tired. But I just can't sleep. I am very sorry. Hope I didn't bother you much."

"Not until now but if you don't sleep, I will consider it as you bothering me. So rest for a while and leave when the sun's brighter."

I took out a bottle from my drawer and handed it over to him. "Here, take a small sip. It will help you sleep."

"What is it?" he said, looking surprised.

"Vodka. It helps in getting sound sleep without a hangover. Try it. Trust me, it works."

Ankit was hesitant, but he did swallow a few sips making a face as though he wanted to vomit. He then lay down on my bed without a word. I spread a thick bedsheet on the floor for myself. After a few sips of vodka, I fell asleep.

The morning welcomed me with a crashing sound. First I heard the door open with a loud bang, and then I heard someone fall. I woke up instantly.

Ankit wasn't sleeping on the bed anymore. My door was half-open. *Ankit must have left already because I do remember locking the door.* I went out to see who had fallen. To my surprise, it was Gaurav – drunk, murmuring something, his voice slurring as if too heavy to be lifted. It was seven in the morning and with only two hours of sleep, my head felt heavy.

I helped Gaurav up from the ground. *Man, he is bulky!* I found the keys to his room in the front pocket of his jeans, which were wet. I could hardly make any sense of his murmurings but as I put him on his bed, he murmured Manish's name.

That night, Gaurav had a high fever. I took him to the hospital. He was dehydrated and was put on saline for a day.

"Did you call my parents and tell them about this situation?" asked Gaurav from his bed, his voice frail and weak.

"No, I haven't. I don't have their number. Do you want me to call them and tell them about this? I am sure they wouldn't approve of the messy 'situation'," I said with a smile.

He smiled back. Six years of hostel life had taught me how to cover up for a brother's mistakes. He leaned back in his bed and stared pensively at the ceiling.

"What happened last night? You had gone out to study as far as I remember. How did you end up like this?" I asked him.

"Don't ask, man. My buddy and I had all but decided to study the whole night when a long-lost friend called up out of nowhere. And we decided to pick him up and drink for old times' sake. But it ended in a tribute to Manish."

"Manish? Why were you guys talking about Manish? You know I am still grieving about him too, and what happened to him was bad but I think we have to move on. Manish would have wanted us to focus on achieving our goal," I said, merely repeating what Sarah had advised me.

"I know. Drinking and thinking about Manish was never the intention, but when my long-lost friend told me his father lived in Samasthipur, I could not help myself from asking him if he or his father knew someone by the name Manish Pandey. To my surprise, his father was the moneylender from whom Manish's dad had borrowed heavily for the wedding."

"Really? So they knew Manish and his family personally?"

"Patience, man," said Gaurav. "As a matter of fact, they didn't know the family personally. But he told me something which pushed me to the brink of depression."

"There's something worse? What is it?"

"My friend's dad had gone to Manish's parents' home to check on their debt schedule. He didn't know of Manish's passing. But after reaching Manish's parents' house, he found it locked. On enquiring from the neighbours, he found that after Manish's death, his father fell extremely ill. Manish's mother is partially blind. His younger sister

Rashmi left town in search of work to support the family. She never came back. That was the last straw for Manish's parents. His father died of a heart attack and his mother committed suicide," Gaurav said in a wooden voice, staring blankly into space.

In my short life, I had never before faced a sorrow as deep and hopeless as the one that enveloped us both. Tears, rants, fury – nothing could provide relief, we knew that. So we sat huddled together, silently. Do we dare call ourselves human? Is this what we do to the best among us? If so, why should I try to be my best? To suffer like Manish and his family? That's too high a price to pay!

"I just couldn't stop drinking the whole night. Why did such terrible things have to happen to Manish and his family? He had not wronged anyone!"

I stared at Gaurav as tears rolled down our cheeks.

"I am going out for a smoke. Do you want anything?" I whispered. He shook his head.

Lighting a cigarette, I called Sarah and told her what had happened. She said she would drop in the next day.

As soon as I finished my call with her, Ankit called. He hadn't called me ever since he left that morning. "I sent your poem to Sakshi, telling her that I wrote it. She read it and instantly called up. We are meeting tomorrow. She did ask me if you helped me with it, but I was able to convince her that it was all me. Hope you don't mind."

"No, you bastard, I don't mind," I said laughing. "I am happy that I could be of some help. Now, please don't lose this pretty girl you got. Do meet her and try to work things out. Less than ten days to go for the exam. Study hard!"

"Thanks, man. Without you, I would have lost her. Where is your exam centre? Sakshi and I have the same centre, some school in Dwarka."

"My Centre is in Jahangirpuri far from Karol Bagh."

"What about Sarah?"

"Her centre is at Nehru place. It is close to JNU."

Phase 2: First Attempt

10

My First Prelims

Mustafa and I had the same exam centre at Jehangirpuri. As the dreaded day approached, I was getting tense. Knowing that Mustafa would be with me was the only silver lining.

On the penultimate day of exams, I stopped studying. I was going to keep calm and pamper myself. The only thing I was worried about was not waking up on time, for I was now in the habit of waking up after 10 a.m. The exam timing was from 10–12 p.m. for Paper-I and from 3–5 p.m. for Paper-II (CSAT). I had to be fresh, and my mind needed to be sharp and focused.

Mustafa lived nearby, in an equally drab building as mine. We were sharing a morning fag and eating chhole-kulche for breakfast. "How are we going to Jahangirpuri tomorrow?" I asked Mustafa. "I was thinking of booking a Meru cab. It's reliable."

"Wouldn't it be expensive?" said Mustafa noted.

"A little bit, but I want to travel comfortably tomorrow. The metro is too crowded and I don't exactly know where our centre is in Jahangirpuri Meru cabs would be the best option, they have GPS."

"True. Ok, let's book a Meru then," said Mustafa. "I got myself some sleeping pills to help me get a good night's sleep. You and I study the whole night and sleep during the day. We are the owls of Old Rajinder Nagar. Aooowwwwwww…" Mustafa howling like a wolf rather than the owl he intended, made me laugh.

"Sleeping pills? Where did you smuggle those from? You can't buy it without a prescription, and the doctors don't prescribe it until it's medically necessary. So…?"

"Yeah, I know, but being friends with a doctor should have some benefits, right? One of his friends is working as an intern at Ram Manohar Lohia and he got me some out of the pharmacy. Do you want one?"

I was a bit apprehensive about taking it. "Yes, I would love to, but… What if I pop in a pill and never wake up?"

"Keep it. Decide later if you want to have it or not. Even I am going to consume it for the first time tonight," said Mustafa.

I kept the pill carefully in the coin section of my wallet. I booked a Meru cab for the two of us for the next morning and returned home.

At home, Gaurav had his laptop open with a big medical book open on his lap and a cigarette in his hand. He had recovered from his drunken, depressive night.

"Mustafa was kind enough to offer me a sleeping pill that you arranged for him," I said.

"Yup. It's very effective, but I hope you don't get addicted to it. Many of us in the medical line do take it occasionally," he said. "But don't worry, I won't be sleeping till six in the morning, so I will wake you up. Will break open your door if such a need arises. And ask Mustafa also not to overdose on it. He is an owl. I just hope he doesn't gulp down more than one pill. I'll wake you up and you wake Mustafa. Done?"

"Thanks, man. Happy you are back to being your jolly self."

"What option does life leave for us if not to laugh at ourselves and our life?"

"Philoooosophiiiical Gauuuuravvvv!"

In the evening, having bought essentials for the day of the exam, I sat in Gaurav's room for a chat and smoke. I had cancelled my tiffin because I planned to visit the Udipi hotel for dinner, one of my favourite places for south Indian food.

On my way back from the restaurant, I called Mustafa. "Hey, you ready for tomorrow? The cab will arrive at Gol Chakkar at 7:30 a.m. Meet me there."

"Sure. I was just getting ready to sleep. How do you feel about tomorrow? Tense?"

"Yes. I am a bit nervous, but excited too. What about you?"

"Same. This exam means a lot to me. I don't want to flunk in this attempt too. May Allah bless us with success tomorrow."

"I can understand, man! Keep calm and be positive. As the veterans of our field say, *You never know which attempt might be your lucky one*! Just relax. Goodnight!"

"Goodnight, bhai."

▼

I set the alarm for 6 a.m. on my mobile and also on the table clock. I took the sleeping pill and then I plugged in my earphones to listen to Fredric Chopin, the great Polish pianist. That's the last thing I remembered. I woke up to the sound of the alarm. "Oh, you're awake already? Slept well?" Gaurav asked when he came to wake me up.

"Yeah, the pill worked like a dream. I feel well-rested and as fresh as a daisy."

He smiled. "Great! Well, best of luck! It's time for my beauty sleep now, see you later."

Can one sleeping pill really do such wonders? I feel like a horse pumped-up on energy! I didn't think the effect would last, so I had a can of Red Bull along with a smoke after breakfast. In my excitement, I completely forgot to wake up Mustafa. When I remembered after breakfast, I tried calling him on his mobile phone, but to no avail.

He did not take my call. The taxi had already arrived and I asked the driver to wait.

I ran to Mustafa's room and started shouting and banging loudly. Soon the neighbours joined in and after a commotion of a minute or two, he finally opened the door with a blank look on his face. He held his forehead as if he had a hangover.

I grabbed him by the shoulders and jolted him.

"What the fuck happened to you?! You have an exam to appear in, and we are getting late. The taxi is waiting, Mustafa bhai! Now please hurry up, we don't want to get stuck in traffic."

He rushed into his washroom and was ready in ten minutes. "I have a massive headache. I took two pills because I was wide awake even till 1.00 a.m.," he lamented. On the way to Jahangirpuri we stopped at a pharmacy and I got him some Disprin. Unfortunately, the medicine didn't work. Mustafa gave his second attempt to clear Prelims with a massive headache.

After the exam got over at 5 p.m., I waited for Mustafa near the gate of the school. I was keen to ask him about his paper. I couldn't find him or reach him on his phone. I decided to wait for a while longer and checked up on Sarah meanwhile. Sarah sounded happy with whatever efforts she had put in. Ankit called to say that he too was confident that he would clear the exam.

I pulled out the question paper and scanned it. There were hardly any questions on current affairs and way too many on environment and ecology. There were no map-based questions either. Questions were lengthy and the options were hardly any help. Prelims Paper-II was easy for me. There were twenty-five questions based on ten English passages which required reading and re-reading. I didn't have any trouble with them but I knew many aspirants from Hindi medium would surely be complaining about it!

The coaching classes would put up the answer key by midnight, so aspirants could evaluate themselves and get a fair idea whether they would be writing the main exam or not. When Mustafa didn't turn up even after an hour, I headed back, straight to his room.

Why didn't he meet me after the exam? Had he left half-way between the papers? Did he skip the CSAT?

Stop assuming the worst! His door was closed but not locked and the lights were switched off. I knocked on his door but there was no reply. I knocked again. I was about to leave when I heard some movement from within.

The door opened and there stood Mustafa with a sleepy look on his face. He switched the light on and let me in. I stared at him but he didn't look me in the eye.

I broke the uneasy silence. "How was the paper? I attempted 89 questions in Paper-I and 75 questions in Paper-II (CSAT). And you? "

"I didn't give Paper-II," he said firmly, directly looking into my eyes now, with a sad smile.

I was surprised but did not to show it. "Why?"

"Leave it."

"Tell me what happened," I asked firmly as I lit a cigarette, took a drag, and passed it on to Mustafa.

"Those Disprin tablets didn't work. Instead, they made me drowsy as hell. I just lost the capacity to think. Somehow I completed Paper-I but I realized that I wouldn't be able to attempt Paper-II. Another year of disappointment, another long wait," he said, blowing smoke-rings at the ceiling.

I felt sorry for him. He should have given the CSAT paper. The questions were easy and straightforward.

"Only two maths questions and elementary aptitude questions!" he said when he saw the question paper. "Damn that bloody pill! I could have cleared the Prelims this time!" He began to curse the pill profusely and then started shouting and laughing like a madman. By midnight when the score keys were out, he was in tears.

▼

I scored 80 in Paper-I and 143 in Paper-II. I didn't know how to react. I was feeling happy because the cut off prediction for general category aspirants was around 190 to 200 and I estimated my score at 223. Being from ST category, for Mustafa the cut off would have been as low as 160 to 170. Mustafa scored 120 in Paper-I. Had he given Paper-II, and even managed to score 70, he would have undoubtedly cleared the Prelims.

"Tonight I feel like drinking. Don't you, bhai? Let's drink, for you are happy and I am in pain. We won't have a better reason to drink," said Mustafa.

I was taken aback. "But you don't drink, remember? You said you can smoke but you can't drink since the Quran forbids it," I said, trying to convince Mustafa.

"Well, Allah wants me to drink tonight. He has made a joke of my life and now he wants me to laugh."

"But it is midnight and I don't think any shop would be open," I said.

This was the last resort to stop Mustafa from drinking. Just then my phone rang.

"Where the fuck are you? How was the paper?" Gaurav almost shouted.

"Paper was good and I am at Mustafa's place."

In a loud voice, Mustafa said, "Ask him if he has any alcohol with him or if he knows of some theka that would be open at night."

"Tell Mustafa that it's his lucky night. I have a bottle of Teachers with me. I am coming to Mustafa's room. Let's celebrate your success," he said, hanging up before I could say anything more.

11

Mustafa's Story

"It's very rare for Alprax to have side-effects. This is the first time I'm hearing of it," said Gaurav in disbelief after hearing of Mustafa's mishap.

We were three pegs down. Mustafa had not said much.

He lit up yet another cigarette and said, "No one is to be blamed for my condition but myself. I wouldn't have come here to prepare in the first place, if not for the way she treated me. She just left me as if I meant nothing to her. I decided to become an IAS officer only to show her that she made a mistake."

"Who are you talking about?!" Gaurav and I exclaimed at the same time. I was surprised that even Gaurav didn't know given that they had known each other for the past ten years.

"I guess it's time to tell you my sad love story. My friends, there was a girl I loved. Her name was Heer Kaif. We both came from the same place and attended school together in Ladakh. We fell in love as children and stayed in love right to the time..." Mustafa's voice choked and he didn't complete the sentence.

He continued, "After 10th standard, I came to Delhi to study while she left for Srinagar for her higher education. Despite this separation, our love burned as bright as ever. I went to Srinagar at every possible chance. Our love grew stronger. After my graduation from St Stephens, I decided to join my dad's construction business.

"He was a fervent patriot. Serving the nation was the only prestige he wanted me to earn. Since I was the brightest amongst my brothers and sisters, my father expected me to earn the laurels.

"I had my heart set somewhere else. My only goal in life was to become Heer's husband. But Heer was ambitious and wanted to become an IAS officer herself. I didn't want her to go to Delhi as I wanted to marry her right after graduation and settle down in Kargil.

"She said, 'Even if you don't fulfil your dad's wish, I would. Imagine how proud he would be to have a daughter-in-law who was a Civil Servant!' She promised me that right after she cleared UPSC, she would marry me. I yielded.

"Her dad ran a grocery store and couldn't afford to pay her tuition and living expenses in Delhi. Hence, much to my father's disappointment, I joined my father's construction business. I worked hard to make enough money to send to Heer every month. After two attempts, she cleared UPSC and made it into IRS. She was delighted and so was I, thinking we could finally marry and settle down.

"She postponed the wedding again saying she wanted to attend the six-month foundation course at Lal Bahadur Shastri National Academy of Administration (LBSNAA) first. I yielded once more. Soon after she joined the course, her behaviour started to change. She treated me as if I was uncivilized and inferior. She wouldn't answer my calls or messages and would give her busy schedule as an excuse. I was confused and upset, so I paid her a visit at her Academy. When I reached, I gave my name to the guard and said I wanted to meet Heer Kaif. He called her on the intercom. She told him she did not know any Mustafa.

"I entreated him to let me meet her for five minutes but he threatened to call the police if I didn't leave immediately. I was shocked. Six months later I found out that Heer had married a Muslim IPS officer from Lucknow."

There were so many stories doing rounds at Old Rajinder Nagar of how marriages are ruined and romances end when selected aspirants join LBSNAA. Some aspirants call LBSNAA as LOVSNAA, which stands for LOVE + VASNA (love and lust)! Mustafa's story was an example. He blinked away the tears.

"The very next day I decided to leave for Delhi to prepare and become an IAS officer myself. I wanted to prove to her that I wasn't some uncivilized mutt."

After a long silence, Mustafa lit another cigarette. He was smoking like a chimney!

"But just look at me! She cleared her Civil Service Exam in 2008 and here I am, not able to clear even the Prelims."

"I have neither been able to fulfil my dad's wishes nor shown Heer what a big mistake she made by not marrying me."

"Doesn't matter if I won't be able to clear this year. I will clear it next year, I will, Inshaallah…!" he declared passionately, beginning to sob.

I didn't have the heart to tell Mustafa that his desire for revenge was a misguided reason to win the IAS exam battle. Things may have worked out but he had worked for the exam because he wanted to be an IAS officer, not because he wanted to show someone down.

Would Heer even care? She has been married for three years and must have moved on. Here was Mustafa still hooked on to the past, seeking revenge. The waste, the sheer pathos of it smote me.

"*Before you embark on a journey of revenge, dig two graves*," said Confucius. How apt it seemed for Mustafa!

The next morning, I was the first to wake up. It was eight in the morning and Gaurav and Mustafa were still sleeping soundly. I decided to leave for my room without waking them up.

Tired and dizzy because of last night's drinking, I decided to enjoy the pleasure of sleeping for a few more hours in my own bed. So I switched on the cooler and fell asleep, only to be woken up in the afternoon by a loud bang on my door. It was Ankit.

12

A Day Out with Ankit

With my eyes still heavy with sleep, I let Ankit in, too sleepy to respond to his hello. Groggily, I rubbed my eyes. I noticed Gaurav's door was still locked.

"Sorry, I should have called first. I had come down to join the Test series for General Studies for Mains so I thought I'd drop by," Ankit said.

"Hmm! I will also be going for it, but not for the next two days. I will relax and then start my preparation."

"Same here. Want to hang out somewhere?"

"Where?" I asked.

"You tell me?"

"Dude, I don't know much about Delhi, you do. You suggest someplace."

"Let's go to Hauz Khas Village then, since it is beautifully cloudy today."

This was my first visit to Hauz Khas and it seemed like a colourful place with a certain hippie air to it. There were lots of cafés, coffee shops, hookah bars and many foreigners.

We made our way through the garden to the lake. While we were walking along the pond, Ankit asked me, "Would we be able to clear this exam in the first attempt? What do you think?"

"Man, if only I knew, life would be simpler. I hope we do. An astrologer told my dad that Civil Services is on the cards for me! What relief!"

"Do you believe in astrology?"

"I don't, but my parents do."

"Although I have the full support of my parents and no pressure at all, I will have to clear this exam at any cost," Ankit was vehement.

"Don't put so much pressure on yourself, man. Let's enjoy the weather."

"We have the rest of our lives for enjoyment once we clear UPSC," said Ankit, brooding.

"Man, you sound just like my father. He says the same thing. I wonder if a Civil Service job is meant for enjoyment. No wonder our country is suffering because the Civil Servants are busy enjoying their life."

"Well, your father isn't wrong, I think. A year of pain and then just gain, gain, gain," said Ankit, trying to sound rhythmic.

"Well, the sad part is that he said the same thing when I was in 10th standard and then again in 12th standard and then again after Engineering and MBA, and now again he is saying the same thing for UPSC." I chuckled.

There was a long silence. Ankit's face reflected a strange emotion. Then he said, "You know, I suffer from expectations, which are my own creations. Also, I want to marry Sakshi. You know she comes from a conservative IPS family. I have to be at least an IAS to be accepted by her parents."

"Did she say that you have to be an IAS to marry her?"

"No, but I know. Certain things are not said in so many words, it's a given. Plus we don't even belong to the same caste. Becoming an IAS officer would really help tip the balance in my favour."

"C'mon now! She is from an educated family; her father is an IPS. Dude, your dad is Managing Director, Container Corporation of India (CONCOR). Why would her family have a problem? I think it's all in your head."

"Wish I could believe that. Sometimes it's a sin being born in a bureaucratic family. You get a high-end, lavish lifestyle, but you also know it's not going to last forever. The power, the prestige, and the social recognition… I want to give the same lifestyle to Sakshi and our children. My current lifestyle will disappear once my dad retires, the bungalow, the servants, the red beacon car; the perks and privileges; and most important of all…the 'respect'. All of it will go. Including Sakshi, if I don't clear this exam before my dad retires…" he chewed his lip savagely.

I didn't say a word. He had to fight this on his own.

We soon headed to a nice café, where I hogged to my heart's content, but Ankit didn't eat anything. He said his mother had kept dinner ready for him.

After Ankit and I parted ways, I found Gaurav and Mustafa sitting in Gaurav's room. This time with Old Monk.

"IAS babuji is here. Salam Sahib. Bring a chair for our Collector Sahib. Come, DM Sahib, join us," shouted Mustafa. He was drunk and so was Gaurav.

Seeing that, I was a bit hesitant to join them. Then Gaurav said, "So now that you will become an IAS officer, you won't drink with us? Are you showing your bureaucratic traits already? I know how bureaucrats change their colour. You also want to become a *civil serpent?*"

Civil Serpent! It was a funny term and I burst into laughter. It became our thing, whenever I acted moody, Gaurav and Mustafa called me 'Civil Serpent', to remind me that we were friends before anything else.

I also sat down to drink with them that day and the last thing I remember was falling asleep listening to 'Stairway To Heaven' playing on YouTube.

▼

I woke up to the vibration of the cell phone in my pocket. It was Sarah. I was supposed to call her last night.

"Good morning. Why didn't you call me last night and why were you not picking up my call all night?" she asked, calmly but firmly.

I looked at the screen of my mobile and realized there were 11 missed calls by her. "Sorry. I was terribly tired last night when I reached home and then I was forced to drink with Gaurav and Mustafa."

"Okay. Can we meet today?"

"Sure," I said my voice bouncing. "By what time would you be here?"

"No, not your room. I want to go out. Let's visit some quiet, historical place."

"Historical places are not quiet. They are crowded. You know they are surrounded by tourists and travellers. The room is the best place to meet."

"Room, room, room. What's wrong with you? I am in no mood to have sex today. I screwed up my Prelims. I am on the edge and all you want to think about is sex! Come down to Safdarjung Tomb sharp by noon. I have something important to talk about."

"What is it about?"

"Be there and you will know." Sarah hung up.

What could it be that was so important? Is she getting married? Is she leaving me?

I got down at Jor Bagh metro station and took a rickshaw to Safdarjung Tomb. There she was, standing with two tickets in her hand. We entered the monument through a colossal gateway that stood in the middle, surrounded by gardens on all four sides. The tomb of Safdarjung, the Viceroy of Awadh, was a masterpiece of Mughal architecture. I felt Sarah's hand slipping warmly into mine.

"I am leaving for home for a few days," she said, looking into my eyes.

"Yes, you should indeed take a break for a week and come back fresh from home and start studying for Mains. When will you return?"

"I am not going home because I need a break. I am not even sure I am going to clear Prelims. I calculated my score, it's somewhere in the range of 180 to 190 and the expected cut-off for general category is 190 plus. The reason I am going home is that my family wants me to meet some guy for marriage again."

"So which bureaucrat's son are you going to meet this time?"

"A politician's son. I tried to postpone meeting him, told my family that I would meet him after clearing UPSC, but they will have none of it. They gave me time till Prelims. I have to go because the boy's family is really insisting for a meeting. They are hell-bent on me coming to meet him immediately. I… I'll be leaving tomorrow," she said, holding my hand firmly.

"Can't you just talk about me to your parents?"

"They won't understand. You know this. My father would not agree even if my mother does," she said.

"Can't you just even try? At least once?"

"I plan to talk about you to my elder brother. He might understand. But I plan to do it after I at least know whether the guy I am meeting is interested in marrying me. If he rejects me, then I can gradually prepare my family to get them ready for the news that I am planning to marry a Hindu. If I tell them suddenly and that too before meeting the guy, whose family is supposedly the best I can find for marriage, they would surely be angry about it.

"On the other hand, if the guy says yes, then I will have no option but to first tell my elder brother about you, who would subsequently tell my father about it and then hope that he agrees without bursting a nerve. But in case he doesn't… in that case…I just wanted to keep you mentally ready for this."

This was something I knew was coming and I thought I could handle it, but I wasn't that strong. After an hour in silence, holding hands and walking in the gardens, we said our goodbyes, knowing very well that it could be the last time we were meeting. I pretended to take it all like a man and act all mature and civil, but back in my room later that day, I cried.

After reaching home, I went directly to Gaurav's room and saw Mustafa also sitting there, still grieving about his Prelims fiasco.

"Here comes the Civil Serpent! Where are you coming from? Don't waste your time…start studying!" Mustafa said jokingly.

"Sarah is going home to see a prospective groom. I don't know what to do," I burst out.

"Let her go! Don't you waste your time on these girls! They are thankless and merciless. You know how Heer screwed me up. Focus on UPSC. Once you become a Civil Serpent, many more such pretty nagins (female serpents) will come to you on their own," Mustafa shot back immediately.

"I think we are going to drink again tonight," Gaurav joked, hoping to lighten my mood.

"I'll go and get mutton from the bazaar. Let's cook today. I know you love my cooking. I hope it eases your pain," Mustafa offered.

"You don't need to take so much trouble, Mustafa. We can order in. Let's drink to our pain."

After an hour, we found ourselves again drinking for the third night in a row. Tonight we were also feasting on the scrumptious mutton curry Mustafa had cooked for us.

13

Balram Shukla

It was 15 June 2011. Three days had passed since the Prelims got over.

The schedule for Mains would be out only after the Prelims result was declared sometime in August. Expecting to pass the Prelims, I had to get my act together and start preparing for the Mains.

The Mains would begin from 29th October. I had roughly four-and-a-half months to prepare. I decided to join all the test series possible for Mains.

I had it all planned, and I was satisfied with it. As I made my way back to my room after paying the fees for the various test series, I could see that Manish's room was being cleaned.

"New neighbour is coming, dude," the owner told me in passing.

I entered Gaurav's room to give him the news. "Hope he told him about Manish," Gaurav said.

Shaman walked in just then and said, "Avoid talking about Manish. It's creepy to occupy a room whose last occupant had died in tragic circumstances. As it is the pressure of exams is awful. This additional information might affect the new tenant psychologically."

"Okay," said Gaurav. From the way his eyes narrowed, I knew he was annoyed.

"I hope everything is fine? I have asked the plumber to look into the leakages in the kitchen. The electrician will come in the evening to change the tube-light in your room, Gaurav. Let me know if you need anything more. By the way, the first-floor tenants were complaining about some girl visiting frequently. I don't mind you guys inviting your girlfriends. Just ask them not to make a noise while coming up the stairs," he smiled at us slyly.

The new guy who came was Balram Shukla, deeply religious. He prayed thrice a day with the energetic ringing of a brass bell. Since each prayer session was twenty to thirty minutes, those bells soon became a headache for Gaurav.

After Manish's death, Gaurav had changed his studying schedule. He would study the whole night and sleep at 6 a.m. As soon as Gaurav lay down to sleep, Balram's prayers would begin.

"Balram bhai, can you get done with your prayers before 6 a.m.?" he asked Balram at last. "I go to sleep at six and you start ringing the bell at seven. Can anything be done about it?"

"Prabhu, Prabhu! You are awake the whole night? Don't you know that from midnight to 4 a.m. is the time when evil and mischievous spirits emerge to distract you and fill you with terrible thoughts? You should sleep early and wake up early," said Balram piously.

I don't blame Gaurav for doing what he did. He told Balram about Manish. Initially, Balram pretended it wouldn't bother him. But Gaurav had read Balram right. Balram verified Manish's story from me. I was more than happy to confirm everything that Gaurav had told him.

Within a week, Balram shifted into the room next to mine. He didn't mind having to pay the extra three thousand rupees for a twin occupancy room. He told Shaman he wanted an AC room and that's why he was shifting. He didn't tell Shaman the real reason.

Balram and I became good friends. I happily slept through his prayer bells which became progressively louder and longer as the Mains drew close. Balram had taken the Prelims exam while he was working with Accenture. He quit his job when he felt he would clear the Prelims. He came down to Delhi to prepare for the Mains.

"This is not my best attempt. I just gave the Prelims casually and I think I will be clearing them because of CSAT. Let's see if I get lucky in Mains this year. Otherwise, I will give the next attempt with complete preparation."

I asked him, "Which optional subject are you planning to take?

"Public Administration and Philosophy," he said.

"Hey, even I have Philosophy, but why did you choose the subject?"

"Philosophy, because it is not a very vast a subject to study, and Public Administration because I will get insights from my father."

"And what's your Father? Is he a bureaucrat?"

"MLA in Chhattisgarh and leader of opposition in the legislature."

"Wow!" I said, involuntarily. *No wonder Accenture hadn't forced him to serve his notice period!*

14

Night Study

I was missing Sarah. I still hadn't given up on our relationship. I tried calling her many times but she didn't receive my call. *Perhaps things did go in the dreaded direction and she's all set to get married to that politician's brat. Oh god! Will I never get to talk to her again, to see her again?* The thought of it was killing me.

The preparation for UPSC Civil Service turns people melancholic and morose. My self-esteem had taken a nose-dive already. To that frustration, now I had to deal with losing Sarah. My despondency deepened more than ever. Although Gaurav and Balram were dear friends, I felt alienated from them too.

My increased consumption of cigarettes, Red Bull and porn helped me blunt the edge of my frustration a little and focus on Civils preparation. The various test series made my schedule very hectic.

▼

When smoking and porn could no longer keep me focused, I thought a study companion would help me stay motivated. I wanted to study with Gaurav, but we would more often than not start chatting about love, life, philosophy and hell of a lot of other things. Mustafa went home to Kargil for a month. I was on the lookout for a new partner; an ideal candidate would be someone who had psychology as a subject too.

Luckily, I remembered Indu Reddy – a fellow aspirant who was with me in KSG. She had once asked me about my preparations for Psychology and would ping me sometimes on Facebook to know which books and notes the teacher had suggested.

"Hey, Indu. Wassup? How are you? How did you do in your Prelims?" I left a message for her on Facebook.

She was online at the moment. "I am fine and in Delhi. Arrived two days ago from Bangalore. I am expecting 190 plus in Prelims. I am quite hopeful about clearing the exam but let's wait and see. Planning to study Psychology and at least finish Paper-I before the results are out. I will need your help with that."

"Oh, what a coincidence! I pinged you today because I was looking for a study companion too. I will help you as much as I can but I will also need your help. I remember you did MA in psychology from Lady Shri Ram, right? You can help me clear my basics."

"C'mon, you're being modest," she wrote.

"Oh no! Pathak Sir dictates so fast. I just couldn't keep up with him. Would you believe, I paid thirty-five thousand rupees for the tuition, and yet I Xeroxed Psychology class notes of someone else who wrote legibly?"

"Don't worry. We will help each other out."

"I wanted a partner for late-night studies. Hope you are not against all-night study sessions?"

"No, I am not. I can only study at night. So when do you wish to start?"

"Tomorrow, it is a Monday. Every Sunday I have a Psychology test series. I will need to finish the syllabus for the test series by Friday, revise it on Saturday and give the test on Sunday. Then I must prepare for Philosophy and General Studies Test series."

Indu texted, "My God! Will you be able to sustain such a hectic schedule?"

"Red Bull Zindabad!" I wrote.

"Costly pleasures you have."

"Papa Zindabad!"

"Hahahahaha :P :D ;-)... see you, tomorrow dude...my number is 8896589655...send me yours..."

"9998563268. Goodnight. See you tomorrow."

I felt slightly guilty that night. I vaguely felt that studying at night with a female companion was like cheating on Sarah!

Should I care since she was the one who had been ignoring my existence? What if I just didn't tell her? Would that be mean? I somehow justified that it was okay to study with Indu. *It's just society that has got things wrong. Can't a man and woman just be friends?*

▼

I was in Indu's room the next night at 10 p.m. Her room was a few blocks away from mine. Where most wouldn't be okay with late-night study with a guy, Indu was welcoming.

"Just give me five more minutes, need to finish this call," she said walking out into her room's balcony. Her room was sparsely furnished, but had an AC, a luxury for many. She had spread a thick mattress on the floor. I wondered if she wanted me to sit on it or on the bed? I waited for her to finish the call and occupied the chair till then. I could hear her. Her voice rose higher, it seemed she was arguing with someone. *Who could it be?* Before I could try and guess, she was done with her call.

She forced a smile on her face. "Sorry. It was my dad on the phone. Hope it wasn't difficult for you to locate my place."

"Is everything alright between you and your dad?" I asked out of curiosity.

She ignored my question with a smile and sat down on the mattress with her back against the wall.

"Hey you sit on the bed, and I'll sit on the mattress," I said.

But she insisted I sit on the bed. She said, "I am good with Applied Psychology but not good with the statistics part. I like Cognitive and Behavioural psychology. What are your strong points in Psychology?"

I looked clueless. I didn't know what to say.

Gosh, I don't even remember the syllabus or the name of the psychologists! I only remember Freud because all he does is relate everything to sex. Why do you eat? Sex. Why do you sleep? Sex. And why do most men have their father as a role model and most women have their mother as a role model? Same answer, sex. While growing up, children have sexual feelings for parents of the opposite sex. God, that was disgusting in a way! This was what made me smile cynically when people said that their mother or father was their role model.

"I know a little bit from each topic of psychology. I really need to revise. My fundamentals are weak," I said apologetically.

She said, "You should study and revise hard. I hope I can be of some help."

I sat on the bed with my back against the wall. "We'll both be at LBSNAA, Mussoorie. Now let's study."

We charted up a plan and sat studying until 4 a.m., punctuated with a couple of half an hour breaks for Maggie and tea, which Indu prepared in the kitchen. These late-night sessions for studies with Indu turned out to be very productive for me.

15

Sarah Returns

My preparation was at its peak and I had begun to get used to the idea that Sarah would never return. Moreover, Indu and I had started to enjoy each other's friendship. She was also going through problems of her own. Her relationship with her father was vocally violent.

I would bump into Ankit every now and then. One day I was returning from Standard chole-bhature wala after breakfast when I ran into him.

"Test series?" I asked after we said our hellos.

"Yes. It was from 8 a.m. to 11 a.m."

"How's the prep going and how is Sakshi? Hope everything is fine with her?"

"Things are much better with me and Sakshi. We meet regularly and spend time together. She is also expecting to clear the Prelims, so now she's focused on preparing for Mains." Ankit said cheerfully.

"That's good, man. How much is she expecting in Prelims?"

"Around 213, I think."

"That's nice. I am so happy for you. Hope you both clear the exams together and get married."

"I don't know about her, but even if I clear IAS and she doesn't, that would also be enough for us to marry. Hopefully!" he said, smiling mischievously. "What are you planning to do now? I want to take a break this afternoon. You want to join me?"

"Don't you want to meet Sakshi?"

"She has gone on a week-long holiday."

"Okay, sure. Let's go to my room. I'll change and we will leave. But where exactly are we going?" I asked.

"Hauz Khas Village. The lake and the ducks are calling us again for a leisurely walk. Let's relax there and talk about love and life like last time. Then we can go have hookah at Maquinas. Or you can have a beer or two."

▼

Our stroll along the lake wasn't as relaxing as I hoped for. Ankit decided to open up like a charged-up can of soda and started decanting his anxieties all over me.

I heard him out. Once he had let off steam, he said, "Sorry for biting your ear off. I really have no one else to share these things with."

No one else? He's lived here his entire life and has no one else? How introvert has this guy been? Actually, I don't recall Ankit ever talking about any of his other friends. Nobody can place him at KSG, even Sarah and Indu have heard about Ankit only from me. Can't blame them, nothing about him stands out in a crowd of three hundred students. Maybe he's very good at being a loner.

I was about to ask Ankit to relax and focus on his studies when I felt my cell phone vibrating. *It was Sarah!* My heart officially jumped into my mouth.

"Hello. How are you?" she asked.

"I thought you would never call."

"I am sorry. Can we meet? I want to talk to you in person. I'll come down to your place in the evening at around six, if you don't mind?"

"Sure. See you at six!" I said.

"Who was it?" Ankit asked, unaware of my uncertain relationship with Sarah.

"Sarah," I said. "She had gone home, and is now back. Have to meet her in the evening."

"Where?" Ankit was getting curious.

"At my room."

"Oh, so you guys sleep together?" he grinned, nudging me with his elbow.

▼

I knew it was exactly 6.30 p.m. because I could hear Balram's prayer bells. He prayed at precise times and this was his last prayer of the day. I heard a loud knock on my door. I rushed to open it. It was Sarah!

"What took you so long? I've been knocking for almost two minutes. And who is ringing these bells?" Balram too opened his door to see who was banging on my door so loudly.

I introduced them to each other. Sarah said hello; Balram folded his hands in a namaste and bowed his head before going back in.

"Now who is this new cartoon? The last one was satyawadi Harishchandra and this guy looks no different," Sarah commented. Her comment about Manish was rude and disrespectful.

"He is our new neighbour from Chhattisgarh. His dad is an MLA and opposition leader in the State Assembly. He is a very religious guy."

"Why does he want to become a Civil Servant then? Less money in politics?"

"C'mon now, not everyone is corrupt. Don't see people in such a negative way."

"I am just trying to be sarcastic. Lost your sense of humour since I have been gone, huh?"

"I have been in terrible pain since you have gone. Why didn't you ever answer my calls?"

"Because I wanted you to miss me. I wanted to see how much you could hold on to my absence. Did you start hitting on someone else?"

"Are you mad? It's just been fifteen days. Do you think I am that desperate? You know how madly I love you." My thoughts did venture towards Indu being my study partner. I hated myself for not telling her that, but I thought since I was doing nothing wrong, I need not. "What about you? Did you meet your soon-to-be husband?"

"Yes, I did meet a boy who is never going to be my husband. I rejected him. That guy was a total waste. He is happily lost in the many addictions that he feeds with his dad's money. He barely managed to obtain a Bachelor's degree. My parents advocated for him, said he will improve, become more responsible after marriage. They were impressed with his family background but I refused flatly."

"They didn't protest?"

"They did. Asked me if I was in love with someone."

"What did you say?"

"I said no. I just told them the guy is not the kind I want to spend my life with, simple and straight."

I had mixed emotions, to be honest. "I glad you turned down the proposal. But why didn't you tell them about us? At least your brother?"

"I wanted to, but are you ready for marriage? I mean, mentally ready? Can you call your father right away and tell him that you want to marry me?"

She had a point. I had just five hundred bucks in my pocket and another 10,000 in my bank account. I was jobless. I didn't know how long it would take for me to clear UPSC.

Sarah continued, "That's why I am saying, let's take it slow. I am not getting married now. Let's get financially stable and then think of marriage. I am not going anywhere."

"What if I don't clear Civil Services ever?"

"It doesn't matter to me. You can easily find some government job or private sector job and then marry me. We will have to plan things or else you have to let me go. You can't just expect me to be your girlfriend without having any intention of marriage."

I unfolded a piece of paper on which I had written a poem on the pain of missing her. I handed it over to her.

"Another poem? So sweet. Let me read," she said and started reading silently.

BROKEN VOWS

Come my dearest, come my darling,
Come, the Pir of Baroque Mosque is calling,
Come like the bride on whom the white roses are falling,
Oh, come just to break your vows again…
Come like the memory of the forgotten,
That lines up in silence,
Come out from your graveyard,
Dug deep within my heart,
Oh, come on a gentle winter Vivaldi violin tune,
Like a subtle remembrance.

Come my maiden to the silent convent,
Hidden deep within the mountain of saints,
Come my maiden to the medieval bell,
Near the Romanesque village wishing well,
Oh come I wait for you lonely here,
Oh, come just to break the vows you made there.
Come and infect me,
With the happiness you suffer from.
Come and bring me,
To the point of tears.
Come and haunt me,
I wait here lonely.

Oh, come just to break your vows again.
She turned to me, overcome.

"Baby, this is incredibly romantic. I am blessed to have such a loving boyfriend. I am terribly sorry to have put you through so much pain. But on a lighter note, you write such good poems when you are in pain and you fuck so well when you are anxious or sad. I think pain and sadness suit you," Sarah said.

Then she gave me a chaste peck and announced, "I am leaving. Have some work early tomorrow morning. Have to make a presentation for my M.Phil."

"It's at 8.30 p.m. Don't you think it is late? You will miss dinner. Eat something here and go."

"Don't worry, I will eat on campus. You focus on your Mains. My chances are 50-50, but I will still start Mains preparation from the day after tomorrow."

I went to drop Sarah at the Karol Bagh metro station. While returning, I saw Indu with Rohini near KSG.

"Hey, where are you coming from?" asked Indu.

"Had gone to drop my girlfriend at the metro."

"Oh, I thought you guys broke up…"

"I know. But she turned up today and had a reasonable explanation for all of it. So, things are better now. What are you doing here?"

"I had to pick up some book from Kumar's. This is my friend Rohini. Hope you know her?"

I said, looking at Rohini, "Yes, I do. Rohini was in KSG with us, right? I have even spoken to you about some doubt I had in class."

"It was regarding polity, I remember," she replied.

"Oh, yes! It was regarding Article 21 and gay rights." *How could I forget that discussion?*

"Yes and I told you how even though it is against the right to leading one's life as one wishes, but still it is against our culture…and then we had a discussion."

"Yes and that other guy..."

"That other guy is Abhijeet and he is my boyfriend," said Rohini firmly as she cut me short.

"Yes, Abhijeet, I am sorry. I remember he also tried to justify that homosexuality is against our culture. Well, that was a year ago. By the way, I had a friend in Symbiosis who was gay. I saw how he was being treated by others for no apparent fault of his."

"He needs treatment," she said.

"I wouldn't like to start another debate here."

"Friends, leave it for the government to decide," said Indu, interfering before the initial pleasantries turned into another argument.

"So how was your Prelims exam, Rohini?" I said, changing the subject.

"It was good. I will clear."

"Well, that's good. All the best with the Mains preparation," I said, as she waved us goodbye.

"She doesn't like me, it seems," I said to Indu, as we watched her leave.

"Maybe. I think it's just that you guys don't know each other. Don't worry, next Sunday, we are planning a small party at our place. You will get more familiar with her and her boyfriend."

"That would be good. But she drinks?" I asked slightly surprised.

"She does, but only when her boyfriend is around. He is the one who gave her the vice."

"Interesting. Anyways it's already 9 p.m. Come, I'll get my Psychology notes and then we will head to your room," I said.

On the way to my room, I still wondered if I should have told Sarah that I study at Indu's place and sleep there too. I didn't want her to think that I didn't wait for her and fell for another woman.

16

The Prelims Result

Unlike other days, today was different – fresh with hope and positivity.

I woke up pretty early, feeling well-rested. I planned to clean my room, get rid of the cobwebs; take down my books and notes off the wooden rack and give it a thorough clean up.

To my surprise, everything was already spotless and organized. *Did Sarah clean my room? I don't recall her coming here in the last fortnight! Maybe I cleaned the room!* I couldn't remember.

She had often complained about my room smelling bad and that my washroom was dirty. I went to check it and voila! The washroom was transformed too! It smelled of lemons. No hair clogged the drain and the toilet seat was surprisingly dry.

What has happened to my room? Should I be concerned about it? Am I just overreacting? Why couldn't I remember anything about yesterday? I was feeling so free and light. Was it because I had no memory of yesterday? I decided to enjoy myself and go for a walk to enjoy the morning air.

On my way out I noticed that Balram's and Gaurav's rooms were locked. As I walked down the stairs, I saw the staircase was well-lit. The building in Old Rajinder Nagar all had narrow, pokey staircases which needed artificial illumination even in the day. *Looks like Shaman has finally replaced the fused bulb with new ones, after my constant complaints!*

To my surprise, I saw no dogs on the streets. *Where are the dogs?* I had complained to the Delhi Municipal Corporation about the stray dogs.

After an hour of jogging in the park, I went for a cup of chai to the only shop opened at 5:30 in the morning in Old Rajinder Nagar. The old man smiled at me and asked me where I had been for the past few weeks. I just nodded and smiled back. I bought a packet of Maggi from him. He also had packs of Classic Mild, but I had no recollection of their taste nor the urge to find out. I felt so fresh and energetic as if I already had ten cans of Red Bull.

Reaching home, I found a guitar propped up in the corner of my room. I had no memory of how the guitar came in my room. *Had Sarah gifted it to me?* I remember my father was strictly against me taking my guitar with me to Delhi. We both knew there won't be much studying if I had it. But I didn't care to think anymore. I was holding a guitar in my hand after a very long time.

I started to strum slowly, thinking that my neighbours would wake up but then I remembered they were not in their rooms. I took out my poem book and turned to one called 'Button Nosed Little Punk'. I had written it for a girl named Natasha, in college. I read the poem and tried to remember the chords for it. Finally, I got the chord pattern, and I started singing aloud.

Northern lights in the northern sky,
The southern sky is filled by your glow.
There is something on your mind,
But you never seem to show at all.
Your eyes are shining shy,
But you never seem to show at all.
In your room and on your bed,

All the fantasy books that you read,
Is it offering you an escape?
Or are you still searching for a place to hide?
Oh, my button nosed li'l punk,
You never seem to show at all.
All the whispering that goes around,
The way you move without a sound,
All the rules that you lay down,
Wears me out, it's just breaking me down.
Your innocence is running wild,
But you never seem to show at all.
Your eyes are shining shy,
Your infantile mind is getting high.
Oh, my button nosed li'l punk,
But you never seem to show at all.

A friend had helped me out by recording this song for Natasha. Natasha loved it. But as destiny would have it, she fell in love with the same friend. Today the pain of losing her to him had drained away. I felt cleansed and happy.

The day was turning out to be absolutely exhilarating.

What was happening? Why did everything feel so right?

When I returned to my room, I sat down to read my favourite poet, Rumi. For over a year I had postponed reading Rumi's masterpiece Masnavi. It was such a beautiful book. The UPSC pressure kept me away from doing the things I loved. But today, I seemed to be spending the day in a way I had always planned to for a long time.

I started reading the poem titled "It's a Beautiful Day to Die Today". It was indeed a beautiful day to die. I didn't remember such a day when I had no expectations from life; everything seemed so easy and blessed. A blade lay on the table within my reach so close that I didn't even have to move an inch from my chair to slit my wrist. But as I was about to slit my wrist, my cellphone began to ring.

It was Sakshi Singh on the phone. I didn't remember exchanging numbers with her, and she had never called me before. Her voice was so gentle and sweet. She seemed excited about something. "Congratulations. I knew you would do it, but AIR 30 and that too in the first attempt. IAS Sahib, well done!"

"What? The results are out?" I just couldn't remember anything! I was happy about it, but now I was also a bit scared.

"Yes. Just minutes ago…" and before she could finish, I heard beeps indicating call waiting.

"Hey Sakshi, I will call you up soon. I am receiving calls from others."

The rest of the night I just got so many calls from so many known and unknown people. But I wasn't feeling happy. I should have been. After all, I had cleared UPSC civil service in the first attempt with AIR 30. I would be an IAS officer.

So many people called me that day. It hurt to realize that I had to become an IAS for people to think of me. Being the person that I am wasn't enough for the world.

I was sad by the end of the day, somehow. I opened my cupboard and found a bottle of Old Monk. I decided to drink alone. There were knocks on my door, but I didn't open it.

I opened the door when I heard Ankit's familiar voice. My head was throbbing as I got up to open the door.

As soon as I opened the door, Ankit jumped on me and hugged me so tight that I felt I would suffocate. Ankit congratulated me and took my head in his hands. He shook it so hard I felt a terrible pain in my neck and I felt dizzy, while Ankit kept shouting out my name in joy.

▼

I heard a girl's familiar voice calling out my name and shaking me by the shoulder.

"Wake up. The results are out!" It was Indu.

"What time is it?"

"1:30 p.m."

What a dream Indu had woken me up from!

The news of the Prelims results being declared brought me back to my senses within minutes. I didn't bother to ask Indu if she had cleared or not; I was too concerned to check my own result. I had saved my roll number on my mobile phone.

"Tell me your roll number," she said. "I have downloaded the results PDF."

"447748," I said, and waited for her to check it. As she fed the number in the PDF search, I could see her face not showing any emotions. And then I saw her lips move. "Congrats, you have cleared."

"And you?" I should have read her emotionless face. But she just shook her head indicating that she hadn't cleared it.

"Better luck next time! Don't lose heart."

She didn't say anything. She wasn't looking for sympathy. The failure rate was high amongst my friends. Sarah, Indu, Sakshi, Mustafa, and Balram flunked. Ankit, Rohini, Abhijeet and I managed to pass.

That night Indu, Rohini, and Abhijeet planned a drink-party at Indu's place. They decided to invite me. "Hey, can I invite Ankit too, if you guys don't mind?" I asked them.

"Sure, no problems," they readily agreed.

"We have heard his name a lot, but never seen him. Tonight we would finally get to meet him," said Rohini.

"Yes, I am also eager to meet him. I have History optional, like Ankit. But I don't remember seeing him at KSG or at the History classes. He must be a low-profile guy. I am sure he will be able to clear this exam in one go. Such guys are very dedicated and hardworking," said Abhijeet.

"Sorry guys! I just spoke to him on the phone. He won't be joining us, said he needed to be with his girlfriend. She flunked and is pretty upset," I later informed everyone.

17

IAS Maharashtra Cadre

When I told my parents that I had cleared the Prelims they reacted casually, as if the result was no surprise to them. It was as if they had known, even before I was born, that I was meant to clear the toughest exam in the country!

There was nothing unconditional about their love. If you obeyed them and chose things that fit into their world-view, only then would you truly deserve their love. The love they tried to shower on me suffocated me. When love is laden with unreasonable expectations and such a deep desire to control, it is bound to suffocate.

There was little more than two months left for Mains. The thought of not clearing UPSC Mains in the first attempt and remaining stuck in Old Rajinder Nagar scared the hell out of me.

The UPSC Civil Service 2011 Mains forms were out. I was super excited and, in a hurry, to fill the form as if filling the form quickly would improve my chances!

It was a lengthy document. The most interesting part was related to the service order preference and cadre preference, that is, which State you would prefer to be in, in case you get IAS or IPS.

"Ankit, help me out with this Mains form, please," I asked Ankit.

"Which part do you need help with?" he asked.

"Have you filled yours?"

"Yes, I have already filled it and submitted online. All I need to do now is take a print out, attach the relevant documents and submit it at Dholpur house."

"Wow, that was super-quick!"

"Help me out with the service preference and cadre preference," I said.

"What do you want to become? I want to be an IAS."

"Even I want to be an IAS," I said.

"Are you sure? The kind of personality you have, I think you should go for IFS," said Ankit.

"And what kind of personality do you think I have?"

"You have good taste in literature, you enjoy Western classical music, write poems and play the guitar. You love foreign language films. You have a charming personality and I remember you telling me that you love travelling. India needs diplomats like you. Go for IFS!"

"No woman has ever praised me as much as you just did, Ankit!" I was pleased, embarrassed and thrilled. "You do have a point. But IAS is IAS. I think I will fill IFS after IAS. The third choice would be IPS and after that?"

"Even I have done the same. I have filled IRS (IT) as the fourth option, followed by IRS (Excise and Customs), Indian Audits and Accounts Service, Indian Railway Traffic Service, DANICS, DANIPS…" And in this manner, Ankit recited the order of the rest of the services.

"Wait! Let me write down the service preference and cadre preference. Did you take anyone's help while filling this?"

"Yes, Sakshi helped me. Especially with the cadre preference for IPS since her dad is an IPS. I also took the help of my dad and his friends, who are in different services."

"Why the hell did you keep crying all the time that you are scared you will fail when you are so confident from within?"

"It was just the Prelims, dude. Anyone can clear Prelims. It was so easy. I mean who fails in Prelims? People should quit if they fail in Prelims," he said with a sense of superiority.

"Not everyone. Just because you cleared, doesn't mean everyone does." I said but changed track soon, "I bet now you will cry until Mains that you are scared of flunking! Then, once you clear the Mains, you'll say anyone can clear Mains. Then you'll start crying about the interview!"

Ankit burst into guffaws. I had never heard Ankit laugh so freely. Mostly he just pretended he was smiling, leave alone laughing.

In my detailed discussion with Ankit, one point that he made clearly was – No matter which service you were in or which cadre you got, to work hard and do well for society (or not) was always your choice. In any service and cadre, you would get plenty of opportunities to show your worth. The choice was entirely yours, whether you wanted to be a Servant or a Serpent.

I decided to put IAS Maharashtra Cadre as my first option. The rest of the service and cadre preference was more or less a copy of Ankit's preferences. I decided to give my first Mains attempt from Delhi, although I was tempted to opt for some examination centre in the Northeast. This was because a few years ago some AIR 1 had opted for Guwahati as the centre and she got outstanding score in Mains.

I had decided I would give my second attempt from some centre in the Northeast if I did not clear it in the first go. Both the centres there - Guwahati and Shillong – were beautiful!

It was quite tempting to appear for Mains from any of these places. But there was an inherent risk to appear from a totally unknown place, so I decided against it. Ankit was already against this idea and so were my parents. Maybe it was in my destiny to clear IAS in the first attempt and then visit Guwahati and Shillong as part of the Bharat Darshan phase of IAS training.

18

The Beginning of the End

UPSC Mains exams were a little more than a month away. I was addicted to everything that I felt would increase my concentration. Red Bull, black coffee and cigarettes, which ruined my sleep cycle. I was fed up of the bland food served by the tiffin service and craved some tasty food.

I began ordering from local restaurants which upset my stomach because the food was cooked in their small, cramped, unhygienic kitchens. My behaviour was becoming more and more erratic as the exam neared, and it was still a month away. I was getting so worried and tense that even talking to Sarah for more than two minutes irritated me. Sarah could sense the change in me. It was more than a month since we had met. We barely spoke for a few minutes on the phone.

We loved each other, but we had nothing to say to each other apart from the usual pleasantries. We fought over petty things more often. Still, we wanted to make it work.

She came over and took me out for a Harry Potter movie. She was trying her best to lighten my mood. I could see the effort she was making. I truly appreciated it, but the fear of impending exams had frozen me up. Moreover, there was also uncertainty about our relationship.

Oh, I did love her. I told her that again and again when we returned to our room after the movie while we undressed. The love-making ended before it started. I had no stamina. I didn't even last for a minute. I was breathing heavily and my thighs and back pained. I reached for the cigarette and saw clear signs of frustration on Sarah's face. I felt guilty and helpless.

After a moment's silence, Sarah spoke, "Do you really love me?"

"What do you mean? Why do you think I am spending time with you?"

"So you get to have sex with me and release your exam pressure, that's why," she said, her voice detached, cold.

"Are you out of your mind? If that was true, why would I spend the whole day with you for just a minute of sex? Don't you think I could self-pleasure myself?"

"But it doesn't seem to be love. I don't feel it. You are just not able to give me time. You never come to meet me. You rarely call, and when I do, you pick a fight at the drop of a hat."

"Try to understand, babes. It's just a passing phase. Once I clear this exam our life will be easy."

"No, it's not going to be easy. After you become IAS, the real fight starts. You know the pressure in such jobs. It's nothing compared to what you are going through now. Political pressure, public pressure, media scrutiny and there would be so much pressure to perform and deliver. How are you going to make a marriage work when you can't manage our relationship now?"

I didn't say anything. The UPSC Mains' untouched syllabus and the unrevised syllabus were bothering me more than Sarah's concerns about our relationship. I thought Sarah would understand that once I cleared IAS, everything would be all right.

As I was caught in this web of thinking, Sarah, sensing confusion in my mind regarding our relationship, asked, "Do you want to break up?"

"No!" I shouted in panic.

I was trying my best to clear Mains with my mind drowning in pessimistic thoughts. I didn't want to lose Sarah! I just wasn't prepared for it emotionally. At this moment, the probability of failing in Mains as well as losing Sarah was pretty high.

"Do you just want to hold on to me without investing your time and love in me?" she asked.

"I don't think I have a straight answer for it. Nor do I think it's the right time to get into all this, as I can't think straight. I am under tremendous stress. All you need to know is that I love you and I want you."

"Then make me feel that way! I feel more and more distant from you every day! You don't even remember my birthday."

"I do," I said hurriedly because that's the first thing that came to mind.

"Then why haven't you wished me all day!?" Sarah said, her voice cold.

▼

Today was her birthday and she had come all the way to meet me!

A debilitating sense of guilt filled my heart. Sarah didn't stay with me that night. She said she had to spend the night at her brother's place in Ghaziabad as they had arranged a dinner party for her. That was the beginning of the end between us.

One afternoon, a few days before the exam, I saw a random number flashing on my mobile. I avoided taking calls from random numbers. The caller was persistent. I decided to take the call.

"Hey, wassup?" a voice said.

"Who is this? Sorry I don't have this number."

It was a female voice. Didn't sound like Sarah, but sounded similar.

Sakshi! How come she's calling me!

"Don't study so much that you don't even recognize my voice," she said with a chuckle. This was the first time she was calling me. The last time she had called me was in my dreams.

"Hello, Sakshi! What a pleasant surprise! I am really sorry, I don't take calls from unknown numbers."

"Nah, it's okay, I can understand. Just a few days remaining for the exams to begin. I thought I'll call up and ask how your preparation is shaping up. Ankit talks a lot about you."

"Really? Hope he says good things!"

"Yes, he does. He says how sensible you are and how well you are handling your relationship with Sarah even during such stressful times."

I felt like laughing when I heard Sakshi say this. If she only knew that I couldn't even remember my girlfriend's birthday and how things were between us at the moment, she wouldn't think of me the same way as Ankit had portrayed me.

"So sweet of him to say such nice things about me. What's up with you?" I asked.

"Just recovering from the shock of failing in the Prelims. I am lucky to have Ankit around for emotional support. I have slowly started studying for my optional subject for next year Mains. I thought of finishing it so that I can concentrate on next year's Prelims from December."

"Yes, you are doing the right thing. You have to be strong. You do know this exam is a gamble, Sakshi. I suggested the same thing to my girlfriend. She too didn't clear the Prelims."

"Why don't all four of us meet this Sunday? From next week, your exams are starting, so let's meet for an hour or something. It would freshen you guys up. Ankit and I are meeting this Sunday at Karol Bagh Metro CCD. Both of you can join us."

"That would be a great idea. I will ask Sarah. She is busy with her M.Phil presentations. If she agrees to join us, well and good, but if she doesn't, I will come for sure."

"Cool then, see you this Sunday. Bye and take care, study hard and don't forget to give my regards to Sarah."

▼

The three of us met that Sunday. I completely forgot to tell Sarah, or maybe I was avoiding her. I can't say for sure.

I wanted to share my worries regarding Sarah with Sakshi and Ankit. They seemed happy together, so I decided to not say anything. The UPSC Civil Service Mains exam was just a week away and this was hardly the time to bring out such issues. Ankit and Sakshi were pretty much in love and it was evident. It showed in the way they whispered in each other's ear, held hands and rested their heads on each other's shoulder. It was very romantic, sitting on the other side watching them.

I missed Sarah terribly. I recalled the early days of our relationship. I wanted us to be like that again. I wanted to rekindle our relationship and infuse fresh energy in it. That night I really wanted to talk to her about us and how we would make it work after the exams were over.

I called her up and waited patiently for her to receive my call. She didn't. It was just 9 p.m. I tried again. Nothing.

I sat down to study, but I just couldn't focus. My mind was filled with the memories of the romantic time I had shared with Sarah and how it would be beautiful once again. I just wanted to hear her voice and assure her that I was not giving up on us. I kept my mobile next to my book and waited impatiently, thinking that she would call as soon as she saw my missed call.

The Mains were a week away and all I could think of was making my relationship work. The guilt of not focusing on Mains and the fear of losing Sarah sent a shiver down my spine.

For the next hour, the hands of the clock moved quickly but she didn't call.

I couldn't bear to wait anymore. I called her again but there was no answer. By then I was in a fit of rage, 100% sure that something was going on behind my back. She must be in love with someone else or why wouldn't she take my call? Like a jilted, jealous, possessive lover, I called up Sarah's friend, Akriti. Sarah had given me her number, for emergency.

Furious, and not bothering to hide it, I asked her if she knew where Sarah was. She did not know. Then I did something that disgusts me to this day. I asked Akriti if Sarah was involved with some guy on JNU campus or if she had again started seeing her ex-boyfriend in JNU. Akriti tried to calm me down, saying she was sure that Sarah would call me soon. I was too incensed to listen to anything.

Sarah called half-an-hour after I spoke to Akriti. It was 11.30 p.m. by then. Unaware of what I had said to Akriti, she sounded apologetic and tried to explain that her phone was on silent mode and she had been busy helping a senior complete her assignment.

I was not in a mood to listen. I had made up my mind that she was cheating on me. After shouting at her for being unfaithful and doing this to me especially when only a week remained for my exam, I asked her not to call me again if she had any self-respect and hung up on her.

By next morning, I felt guilty about accusing her without an iota of reason.

A part of me wanted to make up with her but a larger part still thought she was unfaithful. After three days, the part that wanted to make up and ask for forgiveness, won. I called her and asked for forgiveness, begging her not to leave me. For half an hour I sobbed and made an emotional pitch to her to hold on to me till the Mains, as I would not be able to take the pressure of handling the Mains and losing her at the same time. I made a promise to her that as soon as the exam was over, I would make it up to her for my mistakes and do my best to make our relationship work.

But deep down inside I knew irreparable damage had already been done. Akriti had told Sarah everything.

19

Collateral Damage

The examination day arrived and went, leaving me wondering what happened. I had no idea what answers I wrote and if they were even appropriate for the questions asked. All I remembered was that I was writing non-stop.

I had gone through the past five years' question papers and expected this year's paper to be on similar lines. But like in the prelims, UPSC managed to fox the aspirants again! The number of questions had gone up while the number of options had reduced. Each option would have sub-sections with questions from the polity, economy, nutrition, etc., which were compulsory to answer. Even worse, they made the five-markers compulsory.

I tried tallying up my marks by going through the question paper again and again, but I just couldn't judge how I had done. I had no idea if I would clear the exam. The only good thing I heard from other aspirants was that it was essential to complete the paper, which I had fortunately done.

After the exam I was so burned out, I told my father that if I failed this attempt, I didn't know if I would be able to prepare again. He, as usual, was positive and gave the reference of some unknown, never-heard-of astrologer who had told him that I was destined for an elite *Sarkari* job.

▼

I went home for two weeks after the exam. I wanted to get a dental surgery done; it had been troubling me for a while.

Endless stream of relatives and guests visited me at home, making me feel uneasy. It totally prompted them to make weird comments like – 'When you become an IAS, you won't pick up our calls…', 'Now we will need prior appointments to meet you'. It was all so irritating.

Many of my relatives and parent's friends even told me about random people they knew who prepared for Civil Services for years, but with no success, finally ending up becoming teachers!

My fears multiplied when I heard such talk, making me feel even more depressed. Most of my friends from Engineering and MBA were working in MNCs, drawing handsome salaries. And here I was, jobless, preparing for an exam that might take years to clear.

I was more than happy to be back. Since Sara had been very cold about our relationship in the past few weeks, I wanted to make things better. So, the first thing I did was to call up Ankit. We made plans to meet in the evening along with our respective girlfriends. Ankit and Sakshi were very keen to meet Sarah.

After talking to with Ankit, I called Sarah.

"Hey, I am back. How have you been? Sorry, we couldn't speak on the phone when I was at home," I said, trying to sound cheerful.

"It's okay. How was your stay? And how is your toothache now?"

"Everything is fine. I am just dying to meet you, babe. We are meeting this evening. Ankit and Sakshi also want to meet you."

I was excited to have Sarah meet my friends. I had bought a necklace of beads for her, along with a packet of Haldiram's orange barfi.

Sarah said, "I wanted to talk to you about our relationship. I just don't love you anymore. You are no longer the same person I met at the beginning of the Civils preparation. You used to be a happy-go-lucky guy, but now you have completely changed. You just don't have time for me, nor do you love me. You just want someone to fill your loneliness and this is making you even lonelier. I am sure that until you clear this exam, your behaviour is not going to change. I don't want us to suffocate each other or get hurt." With that, she burst into tears.

After the hard time I had given her, I wasn't expecting her to be happy to hear from me. I knew it was my fault. I wasn't a good boyfriend and she deserved better.

"Babes, let's give us one last try, please," I said in desperation.

"I did. Remember? I took you out for a movie. I even came down to meet you on my birthday and you didn't even remember it. Worst of all, you called up my friend and said such horrible things about me. Just let me go. I am not leaving you because I am in love with someone else. I am leaving you because I don't love you anymore."

"Okay…" was all I could say. I had known it was coming, but I just hadn't prepared myself for the pain.

That night, the first thing Sakshi and Ankit asked me was why I hadn't brought Sarah along. I was not mentally prepared to tell them that I had broken up with her so I said she had gone home for her elder brother's marriage and would return next week.

20

The Interview Preparation

A month had passed since the UPSC Mains exam. I had told Sakshi and Ankit about my breakup. They were both very supportive, and so were Gaurav and Mustafa. After the breakup, I found myself drinking very often, almost every other day.

Plus, when you are stuck in a sad phase, everyone else's life seems to be better and easier than yours. You even become envious of the guy who sells *momos*. The day I found myself moping over how wonderful the *momo*-seller's life was, I knew I was depressed. *Some yardstick that is!*

The Mains result was more than two months away. *Does it make sense to start preparing for the interview? What if I started preparation and found out later that I had not cleared the Mains? All the labour would go to waste. Also, no one knows what kind of questions would be asked by the interviewer.* Other aspirants recommended a thorough revision of the bio-data form filled during the Mains. The probability of being asked a question from it was very high. But there was not much on my bio-data form.

In the *Chronicle*, the competitive magazine for IAS, some IAS topper of an unknown year had said that there was no use preparing for the interview. It was a personality test. You can't build your personality in a month or two.

I was in no mood to prepare for the interview anyway. I was thorough with my bio-data information. I decided to spend my time catching up on all the movies I had missed, along with TV serials like *How I Met Your Mother*, *The Big Bang Theory* and *The Game of Thrones*.

Ankit, on the other hand, had started his preparation. After he begged me long and hard to do the same, I finally gave in. Unlike me, Ankit was highly motivated. I was envious of the energy and zeal he had. His bio-data was surprisingly impressive. His hobby section read: Watching television debates, watching Ramayana and Mahabharata tele-series, participating in debates, group discussions and drama, teaching at an NGO and visiting historical monuments in Delhi.

The section of particulars relating to prizes, medals and scholarships listed many first prizes in various debates and theatre competitions. *Should I be amazed that he secured 99.72 percentile in CAT?*

He was the School Prefect, Captain of Debating and Dramatics Society and Class Representative in college.

I was totally taken aback on reading his form. I had no idea Ankit had dimension to him which went beyond his textbooks.

"All this you have written… is it true or make-believe?"

"Almost all of it is true except for teaching at an NGO and visiting historical monuments in Delhi," he said, with his trademark 'poor-man-crying' smile on his face.

"Dude, what if they catch your lie in the interview?"

"Dude, one of them has been taken care of. My dad has got me a certificate from an NGO stating that I was teaching elementary maths to homeless orphans. And I'll take care of the other one too and you'll help me."

"Sorry, what do you mean?"

"We have two months. Let us explore these monuments together. They might ask you things about Delhi since you have stayed here for almost two years, so…" The smile on Ankit's face was smug as if he had handed me a lifeline.

I was just killing time watching movies and TV serials so gladly accepted Ankit's offer. Going around Delhi would be a great change. Ankit knew various historical monuments, museums, art galleries, libraries and various other heritage sites that Delhi had to offer. So we planned it all up.

Ankit said excitedly, "I will take you to the mystical Agrasen ki Baoli, the forbidden Feroz Shah Kotla, the phantom Jamali Kamali Mosque & Tomb, the traitor Adham Khan's Tomb and the divine Qutb Sahib ki Dargah. I am sure these places will inspire the poet in you."

"Man, you sound like a tour operator now. You don't need to sell these places to me. I would accompany you even if these places were not worth it. It gets so lonely in my room at times and I can't stay glued to the laptop screen the whole day!"

We exchanged a smile. He said, "Sakshi will be joining us too. She will be bird-watching."

"Bird-watching?" I chuckled.

"Bird-watching as in 'watching birds'."

"But is Delhi the right place for bird watching? I hardly see any birds except pigeons and crows here."

"Well, you would be surprised to know that Delhi happens to be the world's second most bird-rich capital city. I'll let Sakshi explain everything else about birds in Delhi when we hang out."

So that Saturday, Sakshi, Ankit and I became the three musketeers with a mission to unravel the stories told by beautiful historical monuments in Delhi; some of which I had only heard of.

▼

On the trip to Agrasen ki Baoli, I decided to carry my notebook in the hope of inspiration striking me to write a poem, as Ankit had suggested. Ankit also carried a shiny red diary to meticulously note down more details about the monuments.

"It is said that King Agrasen during the time of Mahabharata built it and it was later repaired in the 14th century by the Aggrawal community who trace their roots to King Agrasen," Ankit told us.

"So you too are from the line of King Agrasen, Ankit?" Sakshi asked with a smile.

"Evil Sakshi, you be careful. The place is known to be haunted. Djjins live here."

"Not all ghosts are bad, Ankit. You know that." Sakshi said this and started laughing like a little girl.

"What does that mean, Ankit? Have you seen a ghost?" I asked jokingly.

"Have you?" he counter-asked.

"Ghosts and god don't exist. It's just us. Ghost is just a creation of our troubled mind," I said.

Sakshi looked at Ankit and gave him a smile. I could see the love in their eyes. With a pang, I remembered Sarah but shook the remembrance away with a jerk of my head.

It was the middle of Delhi winter. I was having a great time with them as we made our way into the Agrasen ki Baoli from the hustle and bustle of Connaught Place. Fortunately, the place was completely deserted. There were no tourists around. I sat on the steps surrounded on both sides by arches.

Baoli means a stepwell, though there was no water in this one. Sakshi and Ankit sat a few steps ahead of me and Ankit took out his red diary and started making notes. Sakshi began taking photos. For a moment she looked back at me, smiled and took a picture of me.

She looked like a beauty from a bygone era, with a mole just over her lips and a nose-ring. Trust me, to see her in winter, wrapped up in her coat and boots, with her fair cheeks turned pink by the cold, she looked like a princess. I pulled out my notebook. I couldn't help penning down a poem inspired by Sakshi's flawless beauty.

PRIMAL FEELINGS

A beauty that dwells in forbidden thoughts,
That echoes in the pages of myths,
I know that you exist somewhere in between,
The unconscious realm of feelings,
For my heart magnifies your traces subtle,
Your essence found in everything beautiful and gentle.
From seashells to church bells,
They speak about her presence.
For crusades, a many have been taken,
To establish her existence.
Her life still a riddle,
On every philosopher's quest.
But what misses the eye,
Has been caught by feelings.
A lighthouse of hope
In my heart keeps burning,
My eyes dying to see,
What my heart has known for years.
Or am I foolish to give you a physical form,
And enslave you in this world gone wrong.
A feeling that she is of spring making love,
To the trees green and the doves,
The same feeling of lying naked on the grass,
And watch the rain falling from the stars.
A feeling that she is that walks in and slips away,
Like the sand of an hourglass.
Oh, her home, the realm of feelings…

I read the poem over and over. When I looked up I realized I was alone in the baoli, my muse nowhere to be seen. *Where were Sakshi and Ankit?*

I peered to the end of the step-well and could faintly see two people. They were moving still farther away from me.

I went down the steps but the two people disappeared behind the arches of the farthest wall. While going deeper, all that remained was the echo of my footsteps. As this sound became louder in the surrounding silence, the atmosphere turned more mysterious. Worst of all, I recalled what Ankit had said in the cab about the place being haunted.

I felt a strong, eerie presence. I reached the end of the baoli, but Ankit and Sakshi were nowhere to be found. I took out my mobile phone and was about to call Ankit when I heard someone calling my name.

"What are you doing here alone? Don't you know this place is haunted…boo…hoo," said Sakshi.

"I thought you two were down here. I saw someone go down, so I followed, thinking it was you two."

"I told you this place is haunted," said Ankit, laughing, standing close to her.

"You were lost in your notebook, so we went outside to get a bottle of water," Ankit said.

"Let me see what you wrote." Sakshi took the notebook from me and read the poem as we made our way back up the steps. "This is too beautiful. You are a wonderful poet. Who is the inspiration behind it? Sarah?"

I wished I could tell her the truth, still thinking about who I had seen in the stepwell a while back.

"Don't worry, you will find a girl who will love you unconditionally," she said soothingly.

After the somewhat suspense-filled but productive visit to Agrasen ki Baoli, we went to have lunch at Saravana Bhavan in Connaught Place. Ankit then took us to Jamali Kamali Mosque & Tomb, just off the busy

Mehrauli-Gurgaon Road. But by the time we reached the monument, it was already getting dark and the isolated Jamali Kamali Mosque and Tomb reminded me of Agrasen ki Baoli.

"Ankit, I hope this place is not haunted," I said.

"How can a mosque be haunted?" he asked.

"But there is a tomb also in here."

"The tomb is that of a Sufi saint and his lover. Even if this place is haunted the Sufi ghosts are non-violent and peace-loving, so don't worry," he said. And the three of us started laughing.

Indeed, in the limited light of the evening, the place had a divine look to it. The mosque was built like a small fort with turrets and a gateway. Inside the tomb, there were two marble graves with stucco-work and calligraphy.

"The name sounds funny. Jamaliiii Kamaliiiii..." I howled.

"So progressive of the Muslims of those days to have accepted a gay Sufi saint. They even built a tomb and mosque for him and buried his lover next to him."

"Gay Sufi saint?" asked Sakshi.

"Yes Jamali was gay and his lover's name was Kamali," said Ankit.

"Are you sure about this or is it your wild imagination," I asked.

"Always keep your imagination wild or you will never be able to enjoy this dull life."

"Look who is talking. I wish you would practise what you preach but all you think about is UPSC."

"Just a few more months, brother! Then you will see the person I was before UPSC happened to me," said Ankit.

"Amen," said Sakshi.

21

Shit Gets Real

By the first week of March, Sakshi, Ankit and I had managed to cover almost all the famous historical monuments of Delhi, only a few still remained. The Mains result had not been declared, but according to the rumour mill, it could be out any day.

"Meet you in around fifteen minutes. Be there, and don't keep me waiting," Ankit said on the phone.

When I met him a little later, he told me, "Sakshi won't be joining us. Some cousin of hers has come to visit from Mathura for a day or so," he said as we boarded an auto-rickshaw and headed to the nearest metro station.

"I hope the results are not out today, although India Bhai* on Orkut has said it would be out either today or by tomorrow," I said.

*(*India Bhai was an unknown guy on Orkut forum whose anonymous information regarding the date of result declarations and the tentative cut-offs for Prelims, Mains and final merit list had been most accurate and reliable.)*

"Didn't you hear the latest rumour? Someone called up the secretary in UPSC, and he said that the result won't be declared till next week since someone had filed a petition in court wanting cancellation of CSAT and conducting the whole exam again as CSAT is biased towards English medium educated science and engineering graduates."

"If he had to file a petition, he should have done that before Prelims were conducted. Why file it after the Mains and especially when the Mains result is going to be declared. I think it's just some guy having fun. Fuck the result. What's the worst that can happen? We will flunk, right? We are not going to die," I said. But I would be lying if I said I wasn't tense about the possibility of the result being declared today. *What if I flunked? Just have to keep my fingers crossed.*

In the cloudy and cold weather, we made our way through the narrow lanes of some unknown residential society. Soon I could see lichen and moss-laden old walls, obviously a part of some fort.

"Feroz Shah Kotla Stadium!" he announced.

There were not many visitors. Within the ancient fort walls, there were remnants of structures. Some we could identify because of the information board erected by The Archaeological Survey of India in front of the structures, while others were just left nameless. One such structure was a baoli which reminded me of the Agrasen ki Baoli incident and gave me goosebumps once again.

"Hope this place is not haunted like Agrasen ki Baoli?" I asked Ankit.

"Don't worry. Although the baoli here is haunted, it is closed for public. But there are things happening here which are even worse than ghostly experiences."

"What can be worse than ghosts?"

"Religion."

"And how can religion be worse than ghosts?"

"Religion kills a thousand times more people than ghosts do."

I understood what Ankit was trying to say when I started climbing and reached the top. On one side was a structure which was in shambles. I had thought it was a ruin. I realized that whatever was left of the 14th-century mosque was still being used by people to pray. *Wasn't it illegal to use protected monuments for such purposes?*

"Why are you standing down there? Come up." I called out to Ankit.

"Sorry I can't," said Ankit. I couldn't understand why.

Since people were praying inside, I decided against entering the ruins to explore them and got down to where Ankit was. "You didn't come inside Jama Masjid too. Is it something against the religion?" I asked.

"I don't hate any religion. There are good and bad people in all religions. It's just that today I am feeling a bit down and so I don't want to do much of climbing."

Seeing my surprised look, Ankit quickly added, "You see that pillar on top of that stone structure. That's an Ashoka pillar. Feroz Shah Tuglaq brought it from Ambala. It's quite a climb to reach there. You will have to go alone up there too. I have to save energy for the rest of the day."

Why is he acting weird all of a sudden? The structure to climb up was cylindrical and was enclosed by an iron fence. I could see worship material like earthen lamps and incense sticks in the dark little chambers, some of which were locked.

I was on the last layer above which was the Ashoka pillar and I saw people in chambers sitting in the dark, praying to Lords Shiva and Hanuman. This clearly looked like some competition between the people of both Hindu and Muslim religion trying to stake a claim to this place.

It was a historical monument. Why did the government even allow these activities in such places? Ankit was right. Ghosts were more peaceful than these religious fanatics. Whatever little was preserved; these people would destroy it too.

▼

Then we went to Adham Khan's Tomb and Ankit told me all about it. I was surprised how he knew so much, but then, that was Ankit for us! Spending some time there, we made our way to Qutub Sahib ki Dargah. Through narrow lanes filled with worshippers buying chadars and netted garlands from the shops nearby, we made our way into the Dargah. Qutub Sahib's grave lay in the middle of a rectangular enclosure with a dome. The enclosure was entirely covered in rose petals and chadars and netted rose garlands. Worshippers wearing skullcaps and handkerchiefs on their heads were sitting and praying.

Suddenly, Ankit came and whispered in my ears, "Dude, the results are out!"

A shiver ran down my spine. I immediately fished out my phone, typed in the web address and searched for my roll number. I had flunked. I looked at Ankit, he had a blank face as he said, "I'm sorry dude. But if it's any consolation, Sakshi looked up my result. I just received a text that I didn't make it either."

Ankit started to go towards the rectangular enclosure of Qutb Sahib's grave and sat against one of the pillars supporting the dome above. I went and sat next to him.

I switched off my phone and buried my head in-between my legs, with my hands on my head. *Why is this happening to me... Another year of hard work and studying like a dog? Another year of gloomy rooms and struggle with tasteless food in Old Rajinder Nagar? Again the vicious cycle of UPSC preparation would start and I would have to study the same old things. Why!*

I didn't know for how long I sat there drowning in my misery. All of a sudden I felt Ankit tapping on my shoulder. "You know there are many graves within the premises of this Dargah. Among those buried here are the Mughal emperors Bahadur Shah I, Shah Alam II and Akbar II. It is believed that the last Mughal emperor Bahadur Shah II wanted this Dargah to be his resting place. Sadly, he died in Rangoon. Talks of bringing back his remains here have been raised in the past. What do you think? Should they bring his grave back to India?"

"I don't know."

"Come on, what if they asked you this question in..." He stopped abruptly. He hadn't come to terms with the fact that he had flunked in the Mains, but the shock and denial were now wearing off.

"Wish I could dig my own grave here and bury myself right now. Don't have the courage to face my relatives and friends. Can I spend some time in your room?" Ankit said as he got up to leave.

We left the Dargah for my room. I just wanted to hide from the ever-questioning eyes of society. It was good that I had switched off my cell phone and I hoped this would save me from the embarrassment of anyone asking me whether I had cleared Mains exam or not.

The moment we entered my room, Ankit asked, "Do you have something to drink?" Without saying anything, I opened my cupboard and produced a bottle of Old Monk. But as we were about to start drinking, I heard a knock on my door. I opened the door to find Gaurav, drunk out of his senses.

"I am so happy today and I am sad today." He was clearly fumbling. Ankit quietly looked at us. "My school friends are getting married, but look at me, I am still studying to become a doctor. When will I stand on my own feet? When will I prove my worth to my dad? To this world? When god, when?" To my horror, he started banging on Manish's room and started shouting, "Good, Manish, you died. You were saved from your troubles. It's a sin to be born in India and dream of becoming a doctor. Manish, take me along with you. I don't want to live."

I somehow managed to calm him down and put him to his bed. Gaurav sang himself to sleep singing the *3 Idiots* song, "Give me some sunshine," which Ankit and I could hear in my room. It was a dark reminder to us that it was not just the UPSC aspirants who were struggling with their lives.

That night we fell asleep drinking and cursing just about everything about our country; the whole education, economic, political and social-religious setup, everything.

The next day I acquired consciousness at around 11 a.m. I didn't feel like getting out of bed. *What would I tell my parents? What would I say to my friends? I had been jobless ever since I completed my MBA and two years of preparation had gone in vain.* I have found that denial and avoiding confrontation can be comforting, at least for some time. I lay like a log on my bed, immobile and my eyes shut, imagining my troubles vanishing for some time.

Ankit was right, we should have dug our own graves in that Dargah and buried ourselves. Which reminds me, where is he? My eyes flew open. I got up thinking I was on the floor but I realized I had been sleeping on the bed. *Where did he go?*

Somehow I dragged myself out of bed to find my mobile phone. When I switched it on, I had dozens of messages from my parents, relatives and friends. There was a message from Sakshi too, inquiring about the result and asking Ankit to contact her. I tried calling Ankit, but his cell phone was still switched off. I went out to see if Gaurav had seen him leave in the morning.

Gaurav was up already, preparing Maggi in the kitchen.

"Did you happen to see Ankit leaving my room?" I asked Gaurav.

"Who Ankit?"

"The guy who was with me last night when you returned sloshed?"

"Was there anyone with you? Sorry, man. I was too drunk to remember. What happened? Everything alright?"

"No, actually our Mains result was declared yesterday. And we both flunked. He was way too depressed yesterday night. We were drinking together and fell asleep around four in the morning. That's all I remember. But when I woke up, he wasn't there."

"Call him up?"

"I did. His phone was switched off. That's why..." I thought of trying his number one last time before informing Sakshi that I can't get a hold of him. Fortunately, the call connected.

"Where are you?" I asked.

"Home, I just reached. I left your place thirty minutes ago. You were sleeping so I did not disturb you."

"Sakshi messaged me. Call her up."

"Cool, will do it, but first I need to explain to my parents where I was last night and then tell them about the result too. Buzz you later."

▼

Almost half of that day went in Gaurav's room smoking and discussing the mess we were in. He had also flunked in the medical entrance exams. Our common misfortune made us excellent company for each other.

My parents called me repeatedly while solicitations of friends and relatives poured in from all possible channels to sympathize with me. Two or three people even visited my room to make me realize the magnitude of my failure. To their questions, "What next?", "Are you planning to change your optional subject for the next attempt?" and "What is your backup job option?" I had no answer.

Why didn't I appear for the second tier of SSC exam when I had cleared the first tier? At least I could tell the sympathizers that I had a job. I decided to deactivate my Facebook account so people would stop asking me about the results. But even if I killed those voices on Facebook, how would I be able to stop the voices in my head?

Despite the misery, Gaurav and I reached the conclusion that since we had invested so much time in our respective entrance exam preparations; we needed to hold on for another year. It would be painful, but quitting now would haunt us forever.

There was no way out of this quagmire. Going back to a private-sector job was not an option. The kind of non-existent life in the private sector was big enough motivation for me to give this exam another shot.

I even chose to believe the 'statistical fact' that most people clear UPSC civil service exam in their second and third attempt, with most of them in the age group of 26 to 30. *Maybe I should try again. After all, I am just 25 and this was my first attempt.*

By the end of the day, I headed to bed with this happy and rather motivating realization. Just then, my mobile rang, an unknown number flashing on it. Though I didn't want to pick up the phone, I still did.

"Hello?"

"Sarah here. How are you?"

"I am fine."

"How was the result?" she asked, after a long pause.

"Flunked."

"Sad to hear that. Better luck next time."

"How are you?" I asked her just out of courtesy.

"I am fine. I don't know if this is the right time to tell you this, but I am getting married to that UP politician's son."

"Congrats, Sarah! All the very best."

"Thank you. Bye, and take care."

Yes, Sarah, this was definitely not the greatest of times for you to tell me about your marriage. Why did she say yes to the guy she had rejected? I wanted to ask her, but I just couldn't. Male ego. And that miserable day was the last time I ever heard Sarah's voice again.

Phase 3: Second Attempt

22

Resurrection Chant

A week had passed by. All I had done in that time was drown in my grief.

Abhijeet and Rohini paid me an unexpected visit during the week. There is solidarity in misery. We tried our best to shake off our blues and motivate each other.

We decided that between the three of us, we would divide the reading of the magazines and newspapers. It would help distribute our burden. It would free up time to let us revise the information we collect. I picked the *Yojana* magazine, Abhijeet chose *Kurukshetra* magazine and Rohini took up *Economic Times* newspaper. We decided to meet and exchange notes at the end of each month.

"Can you ask Ankit to join us? Maybe he can make notes from *Hindustan Times?*" asked Abhijeet.

"I can ask him, but I am not sure he will join us. I asked him once for group studies, but he was not comfortable with the idea. Said he can't focus. He is an introvert; prefers to keep to himself. "

"I see. But this isn't exactly group studies. Give me his number. I'll talk to him, I hope he has heard about me from you."

"Yes, he has. I once told him about having met you and Rohini at Indu's place. He knows that you were also at KSG."

"I'll give your reference to him."

"Sure," I said.

"Let's go, Abhijeet," said Rohini.

"I'll create a WhatsApp group to keep in touch. If there's an important topic we'll meet up and discuss it, otherwise month-end meetings will be our ritual. We have to crack the exam this time. I don't think any of us can bear yet another frustrating year of this," said Abhijeet, echoing all our thoughts.

"Exactly two months and three weeks to go for Prelims. Hopefully, this time that won't be a problem," said Rohini, grinning as they left my room.

After a week of mourning, it was business as usual, studying twelve-hours a day. I somehow resurrected myself from the depths of self-pity and willed myself to swallow the painful slow poison of UPSC preparation again.

This phase of my life also saw a drastic change in the theme of the poems I wrote. My poems were a mix of dark and intense. Sometimes they were optimistic, a result of forced positivity. The first dark poem I ever wrote during this time was called *Resurrection Chant*, which had a positive message.

Resurrection Chant

In the faceless fields the nameless yields
With time the fallen and forgotten heals,
And very soon the joy of moaning shall begin,
For the rotten happiness of an unapologetic past,
Has come to reside in their broken hearts...

Shall come to pass the weather of failure,
As hopes exposes itself in layers,
What winter loses is spring's gain,
The dawn shall seek the dark again...

Shall rise in silence what are meant to fall,
Failure is only the beginning of resurrection's call,
When the faithless in happiness shall rule all,
The symbols will crumble and love shall gain…

Far away from the living the blessed live,
The Elysian fields are just a grave away,
As sooner or later when the silence falls,
Death is nature's best gift to all,
Where the worthy shall live forever in grace…

▼

The best thing about Old Rajinder Nagar was the support system that bolstered you up when you failed. In this exam the success rate is so low, it's natural to fail and a miracle to pass. Statistics show that the suicide rate is higher among class 10th and 12th students than among Civil Servant aspirants.

From the latter half of March till the first half of May, I spent most my time studying with Balram and Mustafa. Whenever I spoke about my disappointment at not clearing the Mains, Balram and Mustafa would say, "Well, at least you cleared the Prelims. We didn't, so relax! Things would be better this time."

This was just the consolation I needed to push myself through this painful march towards the Prelims. Another good thing about our group? Thanks to Balram, it was early to bed, early to rise for all of us. Our bodies thanked us for a regular body clock.

After returning from home, Mustafa was the same – humorous and full of Urdu quotes. At times his past would haunt him and he would get pensive and melancholic. I couldn't put my finger on it but there was certainly a change in Balram's personality. He was still religious and polite, still had the same small-town innocence and courtesy in him, but something seemed… different.

Once it was just the two of us. Mustafa had gone to his brother's place in Delhi and skipped our group study session. "Hey, I wanted to tell you something. It's personal so let's just keep it between us," he said avoiding my eyes.

"Sure bro, what is it?" I said, bristling with curiosity.

"I...There's this girl I met recently on a train, of all places. Well, we are in love with each other!" he said coyly.

My jaw dropped, "Wow! When did this happen?" I asked, genuinely surprised. This quiet, religious chap was not the most likely candidate for kicking over the traces. Mentally rubbing my hands together in glee, I struggled to maintain a sombre expression. *Balram in love! Balram of all people! LOVE! Oh, boy!*

"We met about two months ago. In this short span, things have become pretty serious," he said, blushing a little.

"Oooh... so this fair maiden is the reason my ever religious Balram has been missing his prayer sessions, huh? Here I thought you are too stressed about the exams!"

He grinned, lowering his eyes like a shy maiden. "Well... yeah... late night calls have been interfering with my sleeping and praying schedules...but I'm happy. This is the first time in my twenty-five-year-old life that a girl not only likes me, but loves me!"

"I'm happy for you, man! I would love to meet her sometime!" I said, enthusiastically.

"Sure!" said he, looking mighty pleased with himself.

▼

With D-day getting closer, tension and anxiety hung heavy around us all the time. Mustafa's sense of humour began to fray, and he became quite irritable. More and more he got embroiled in the 'ifs and buts' of exam results, turning increasingly irritable.

"It's haram to consume alcohol according to the Holy Quran," Mustafa justified why he couldn't drink.

"And smoking tobacco is holy according to the Quran? What kind of logic is this?" scoffed Gaurav.

"Mind your language, Mister. Quran doesn't say anything about cigarettes," said Mustafa, raising his voice. I think Gaurav should have stopped there. But taking liberty with his childhood friend, Gaurav continued.

"Why didn't Allah reveal this in the Holy Quran that cigarettes are bad for health? Did the Prophet Mohammad forget to mention this revelation in the Holy Quran?"

Mustafa stared hard at Gaurav with his eyes spitting fire. His fists were clenched. When words fail to defend, violence takes over.

"One more word and I will break your bones. I don't fucking care who you are, I will beat the hell out of you. Not a single word against the Prophet or Allah!" Mustafa said as he got menacingly close to face Gaurav. Had I not intervened and dragged Mustafa out of Gaurav's room things would have gotten pretty ugly.

By evening Gaurav and Mustafa had apologized to each other and were back on good terms, almost. The fear of failure and the desire to avenge himself on his lost love was making him lose his mental stability. The smallest provocation would set him off on a tirade. I was worried about him. I hoped he would not screw up his paper like he did the last time around. Though he kept on telling me that he was more confident than last year, I had my doubts.

For a change, Ankit seemed to be happier than me. The Prelims were coming closer and Sakshi was cracking up under the pressure. She was dependent on Ankit for emotional support and this dependency made her more vulnerable, which Ankit made the most of with my guidance and poems. In all, Ankit and Sakshi were getting stronger in their love.

▼

Just two weeks before the Prelims, the Mains scorecard was out. It was very unpleasant to know that I scored only 40 marks out of 200 in my

Essay paper. I had missed the Mains cut-off by five marks. And to think that Essay was the only paper I thought I had written well! Instead, it cost me my IAS interview call! I was seriously upset all over again.

The rest of the people who flunked had the same story to tell. Some missed in Optional subjects, some in Essay while most in the General Studies paper.

Honestly, most of my energy had been expended in the first attempt, and so had my zeal and interest. The little motivation I had left was because I had nowhere to go and nothing else to do with my life.

This time, everyone had different exam centres. I warned Gaurav not to give Mustafa any sleeping pills but asked him to arrange one for me. On the morning of the exam, I was responsible for waking Indu and Balram was to rouse Mustafa. The four of us met at the Gol Chakkar, all of us had booked a Meru for 7:30 a.m. Everyone looked a bit nervous, which was obvious.

We all sat in our respective Meru Cabs. My Prelims Centre was thirty-minutes away, at Dholpur House. It was a compulsion with me to reach the examination centre way ahead of time. My cab was about to reach Dholpur house. It was 7:50 a.m., two hours ten minutes to go for the exam.

Just then, Abhijeet called.

"I need your help really bad. The cab I booked bailed on me, man! It's nearly 8 a.m. and my centre is in Dwarka. I tried calling another cab, but can't get any. If you can drop me in your cab, I'll be really grateful to you," said Abhijeet in one go, without pausing for breath.

"Calm down, Abhijeet. Come down to Gol Chakkar. I'll be there in twenty minutes."

"Thanks, man. I owe you big time for this."

I asked the driver to take me back to Gol Chakkar. Abhijeet was standing there sweating. The time was 8:15 a.m.

"Abhijeet, the cab will drop me at Dholpur House. Then you can take the cab to your centre. Is that fine with you?"

"Yes, sure!" he said. That's the only thing he said over the entire ride. He kept glancing at his watch. He wasn't the picture of confidence, calmness and arrogance that I had known from KSG days.

"Call me as soon as you reach your venue," I said as I got down at Dholpur House. He nodded distractedly.

I didn't receive his call before the Prelims started. *Hope he made it on time.*

▼

Sitting in my noisy auto-rickshaw on my way back from the exam, I was 'enjoying' the drone of even noisier traffic. *I don't know why, but I feel I'll clear Prelims this time too. Let me call up others, find out how they fared.*

First I called up Abhijeet. I was relieved to know that he had reached his examination centre on time. He fared better than he expected. Ankit too sounded confident. Mustafa's phone was switched off.

As I reached home, I first entered Balram's room. He was on the phone with his girlfriend and just gave me a thumbs-up. I was happy that he had done well too. Indu and Rohini said they were not sure how they had done and needed the answer keys to get a better idea.

Sakshi, on the other hand, had something weird to say. She refused to calculate her score with the answer keys. "I'm confident I'll clear this time. Now all I need is a break for a few days and then I would directly start preparing for Mains."

I would never do such a thing. How could you motivate yourself without knowing if you were clearing the Prelims or not? Somehow, I had a feeling Sakshi knew she wouldn't be clearing the Prelims this time too. She just didn't want to admit it and wanted to postpone the confirmation. Well, to each his own, who was I to question it?

The keys were out by 7 p.m. on Career Launcher website. I was in the safe zone again. Balram seemed to be clearing the Prelims too. One by one everyone started calling and it seemed everyone was either clearing the Prelims or was on the border.

All of a sudden I received a call from some unknown number. It turned out to be Mustafa. He was using his brother's mobile. "I am getting my brother's car. Let's go to Murthal tonight for dinner."

"Yes, let's go! But how were your Prelims?"

"CSAT wasn't good. I got stuck in the passages. Expecting around 175. Let's hope the ST category cut-off is low. Last year, it was just 165. This year the paper was more difficult. So I hope to clear."

"That's good, Mustafa. Where exactly is Murthal and who else is coming?"

"Murthal is in Sonipat village of Haryana, some fifty odd kilometres from Delhi. Gaurav is coming. Ask Balram too." And by the time Mustafa finished saying this, Gaurav was already on my door knocking and calling out my name.

"I'll be there in an hour. Meet me at Gol Chakkar," said Mustafa.

I went to Balram's room only to find him busy on his phone as usual. "Hey, Mustafa is taking us to Murthal for dinner. Wanna come?" I asked.

"No bro! You guys carry on. I've got plans," he said as he pointed to his phone with a huge grin.

An hour later, Mustafa, Gaurav and I went to Kakey Da Dhaba in Murthal. On our way to the dhaba, we also got four bottles of Budweiser which Gaurav and I had while Mustafa drove.

I felt relieved but not as excited as I was at the thought of clearing Prelims. There was no feeling of achievement.

We had finished dinner and were resting with our back against the car and smoking.

"So Civil Serpentji, this time for sure you are going to clear the exam. Last year you just missed by 5 marks. Now you know how to play this game," said Mustafa.

"No one knows how to play this game. I couldn't figure out what I was writing last year in Mains and never in my dreams had I thought

I would be missing the Mains by just 5 marks. This exam is all about fire and forget. If you get lucky, it's good; else you try again until your attempts dry out or your courage does," I said.

"This is the fourth time I am writing the Prelims and I still don't have a clue how to clear the Prelims. Would I ever clear it?" asked Mustafa helplessly.

"There are so many stories about aspirants who couldn't clear the prelims in their first three attempts, and then in the fourth attempt, made it into IAS. I believe your hard work and patience will pay off, Mustafa." I tried to console him.

All this while, Gaurav was smoking silently, watching the stars and listening to us. When I looked at him, he just smiled, as if trying to hide something.

23

An Atheist Neighbour

After Prelims, I visited home for a week. My parents made me feel as if I had done something wrong by failing in last year's Mains... as if I failed on purpose. On top of that, they were disappointed with my lifestyle more than usual. But their taunts of how I was solely responsible for not clearing the Mains irritated me. Perhaps I shouldn't have minded the things my parents said, but I did. Their words wounded me.

I was at home, but I felt out of place, purposeless and lonelier than I felt in Old Rajinder Nagar.

"We have to attend a wedding tonight. Do get a haircut and shave," said my mother, while chopping tomatoes. She was sitting next to my father, who was reading the newspaper.

"You are now of marriageable age. I got married when I was twenty-four and you are twenty-five. Next year, as soon as you become IAS, you will be married. For that, we must begin searching for a suitable bride now," my father said from behind the newspaper. "There will be many reputable families attending the wedding tonight. So dress well and be polite. We might find my future daughter-in-law there."

Seeing that I didn't say anything, he continued, "Relax. Even if you don't clear UPSC, your father is still alive and kicking. I will get you married and support you monetarily."

I have to get out of this place. My fellow aspirants are happy going home and feel depressed on their return to Old Rajinder Nagar. It was totally the opposite with me.

▼

As I returned from home, I found a new aspirant had rented the room once occupied by Manish. Just as a courtesy, I knocked at his door and waited. I could hear someone reading something aloud, but he didn't open the door. *That's weird.* I went to Gaurav's room. He, as usual, was peeping into his laptop screen with a big textbook open on his lap and a cigarette in his left hand.

"Who is the new guy?"

"Some young dickhead freshly out of IIT Kanpur."

"Why are you calling him a dickhead?" I asked.

"Check out my bathroom."

As I entered the washroom, I could still hear a human voice on the other side of the door, reading something. I looked at the washbasin and the shit pot and found them covered with red stains.

"Is that blood?" I asked.

"Wish it was, at least the stains would go. It's tobacco. Told him so many times not to spit in the washbasin and to flush after spitting in the shit pot, but it's like talking to a wall. All he is concerned about is studying."

"I knocked at his door, but he didn't open it even though I heard him reading."

"He just opens the door for newspaper, lunch and dinner. You might be lucky if he greets you, let alone entertain you for a conversation. I have been to his room once. He has tied a rope just above his study table and he ties it to his ponytail so that his head doesn't fall on the table if he doses off. His room smells like shit. Yesterday he was washing his clothes and I bet even dead rats don't smell so bad," finished Gaurav, his disgust palpable.

I found the situation somewhat hilarious and couldn't stop laughing. "What is his name?" I asked.

"Rajiv Ranjan Jha."

"Didn't you tell him Manish's story? I am sure he would leave the room."

"The only time I visited his room was to tell him the story of Manish in the guise of a courtesy visit. But this guy turned out to be an atheist. He didn't even feel sorry for Manish and just said it's the survival of the fittest and started studying again. I wouldn't have stayed longer either in that horribly smelly room. Don't bother yourself with interacting with this guy. You would be disappointed. He is very cold."

True to Gaurav's assessment, I hardly saw Rajiv in the first month. We crossed on the stairs once but he kept his head lowered and ignored my friendly smile. He always had a *who-has-time-to-be-social* attitude. Only once did he deign to answer when I asked him about his educational background.

Rajiv was a native of Indore. He had graduated in June and had appeared for the Prelims right away. He was expecting to clear it, so he came down to Old Rajinder Nagar to prepare for the Mains. He was just twenty-one, but he looked older. It made me suspicious. *Has he lied on his birth certificate? I wouldn't put it past him.*

This time around, I had decided I wouldn't be joining any test series like last year. Nor would I make a scrapbook of newspapers articles. I would focus on revising as much as possible. However, I realized that I did not have any strategy, nothing exactly new to make sure my score would improve in the Mains. On the contrary, reading the same Psychology notes, Philosophy notes of Patanjali and KSG notes, with even less enthusiasm and efficiency than last year, made me question my preparation for this attempt. I had to do something different, adopt some new strategy.

"Why don't you give your Mains from Northeast or from some different centre? I heard it helps in getting good marks," said Abhijeet.

"Is there any substance in this idea?"

"AIR 1 of 2008 wrote her Mains from Guwahati even though she didn't reside there."

"Are you planning to give the exam from outside Delhi?"

"Yes. I mean what's the harm in trying?"

"But won't there be problems adjusting to the new place?"

"I am giving Mains from Jaipur. It's my hometown so I won't have any problem. You also try giving it from someplace where your relatives stay."

"Almost all my relatives stay in Nagpur. I have one in Ahmedabad, but I don't think I will be comfortable staying at a relative's place for the exam. During exam time I need to have my own space and to have my own schedule. I would prefer staying in a hotel alone."

"Then opt for Guwahati or Shillong as a centre. In the Northeast, I don't think many people prepare for Civil Services. Understand the logic behind why people prefer giving the exam from outside Delhi. Relativity, my dear, relativity."

"But the situation in Assam is volatile. There are riots in the Kokrajhar between indigenous Bodos and Bengali-speaking Muslims who are illegal immigrants from Bangladesh."

"Bhai, then it's even better. Do you remember the riots during 2010 in Kashmir? The topper also came from Kashmir. This time the riots are in Assam," he said with a smile.

Was the Government, as a way of diverting the attention of the people, trying to create heroes in the riot-affected state by making the aspirants belonging to these states top the Civil Service exam? I couldn't understand the logic, but in desperation, I saw it as a sign for my success and my trump card for this attempt.

I pitched my idea to my other aspirant friends. Ankit backed out and so did others. It didn't stop me though. This was going to be my masterstroke. I pitched this idea to my parents also, but they were not convinced. They were scared on account of the volatile situation there.

In fact, I even had a small fight with my father over this difference in opinion. I lost my temper but didn't quite know how I mustered up the courage to snap like that. I guess it was being bottled up in me for years. Taking a stand now was like a breath of fresh air for me. If only Indian parents knew how to accept their kids as individuals, everyone would be a lot happier.

I remember my school education counsellor advised me to opt for Arts based on my aptitude test, but my father asked me to join Engineering because it would fetch me a good job. Then during MBA, he asked me to join Finance when I was more inclined towards Advertising and Marketing. When I was utterly lost during MBA, he suggested I should go for Civil Services.

Right now, I was frustrated and I didn't talk to my parents for a week. Nor did they call. I knew I could go to Northeast only if they gave me money. *Twenty-five and still financially dependent on my parents!* I was disgusted with myself.

Some of my friends probably didn't have the best jobs, but they were happy and living it up their way. I felt forlorn. This was one of the reasons I didn't attend my Engineering College Alumni meeting to be held that week in Delhi. I just didn't know how to answer questions like what I was doing even after completing engineering five years ago!

24

Balram and His Prospective Bride

The beginning of July saw Balram, Mustafa and me immersed in books and anxiety, studying for the Mains. Balram had opted for Sociology and Public Administration as optional subjects whereas Mustafa had opted for Urdu and Public Administration. Thanks to Mustafa, I was introduced to the rich and elegant language of Urdu. Indeed, Urdu tasted even sweeter than wine at times. Whenever Mustafa grew nostalgic, he would give us a treat of Urdu couplets. Balram enjoyed this and he got addicted to Urdu. He started learning the couplets so he could charm his way into the heart of his beloved.

Often, hurdles in Psychology brought me to Indu's for night study sessions. The uncertainty of UPSC exam and family issues back home pushed her more into fagging and boozing, Indu confessed one day. I was battling my own nicotine and caffeine addiction. I did worry about my lungs, but somehow I managed to convince myself that I needed it to clear UPSC. With that, the thought of quitting was easily postponed.

Once in a while, Indu and I would drink together and it was during one such occasion when she got very sentimental.

"Look at my father, he's barely living. My mother died when I was just six years old and my father never remarried. I even asked him to marry for my sake, but he would always say the same thing, 'No one can replace your mother'. He said he saw my mother in me and loved me even more!"

Indu's voice rose as she sobbed. "There are very few men like my dad who would love just one woman and be faithful to her for the rest of their lives. My father dreams of me becoming an IAS officer. How irresponsible of me not to fulfil his dreams but instead be a burden on him! His health is deteriorating day by day and there is hardly anyone to look after him but still, he doesn't want me to leave Delhi. Only because he wants me to focus on my IAS preparation."

"Please don't cry, Indu," I said, passing my handkerchief to her. "It's not over yet. You will surely clear it and make your father proud."

"Yes, I am going to clear this exam for my dad and I won't rest until I do it." She got up suddenly. Barely able to stand, she stumbled into the washroom and took a shower with her clothes on. She came out drenched and smiling.

"There you go! I am happy again. I have washed away my pain."

I left the room for some time so she could change her clothes and she took a long time to do so. She opened the door then crashed on the mattress on the floor.

It was 7 a.m. when I woke up in Indu's room. She was still asleep. I studied for a while then took out my book of poems. I had begun keeping it in my bag at all times. It was my closest companion; a witness to my frustrations or dreams of romance in the loneliest hours of my life. Poetry was always a medium of escape for me. I found my muse sleeping on the ground with her hair across her face. Indu looked like an actress from a south Indian movie. By the time she awoke, it was 11 a.m. and the poem was ready. I decided to show it to her before I left.

"I just finished writing a poem in the morning today. Care to read it?"

"Are you serving me poetry for breakfast? I need lemonade or a painkiller, not poetry. God, this hangover!"

"Come on! I wrote the poem keeping you in mind."The moment I said this, she took the book from my hand and started reading it aloud.

Her Cigarettes and Beers

The way you philosophize life,
With that beer can in your hand,
Lady, such poetry you are when you are drunk,
And those cigarettes in-between your pretty fingers,
You look so very graceful when you smoke,
So very beautiful in the haze,
Like some medieval artwork,
So worthy to be on canvas.

I just love to watch you struggle in bed,
Fighting the sunlight with your pillow,
In all the glory of your Sunday morning hangover,
Innocence oozes out of the drunk look on your face,
And Oh my Godless lady it's time for your,
Lemonades, Novocain and hour-long shower in silence,
I know it's crazy to believe in silly things,
But you look so very pure
When you suffer from your addictions…

"Are you in love with me?" she asked, a sheepish smile on her face.
"No, Indu. I am not in love with you, maybe with your misery."
"I am happy that my sadness inspires someone."

▼

Balram must have heard me unlock my room, he peeked from his room and said, "I wanted to talk to you about something serious. Wanted your advice…"

"Okay… tell me what happened?" I said, inviting him to my room.

"Shalini is asking me to marry her and I don't know what to do. Her parents have found a groom for her." *Oh, so the fair maiden does have a name!*

"Are you out of your mind? You barely met her. You don't even have a job.

"My advice would be to explain to her that marriage in such a short time is not possible. I think you should part ways and focus on UPSC."

"I just can't. She is my first true love. I can't and won't give up on her and my relationship."

"You wanted my advice and I gave it to you. Now you decide what you want to do."

Balram just sat there, his head held between his hands.

"Balram, you hardly know anything about her family or her past. It's just been four months since you met her. Take it slow, brother."

"I just can't sit here and watch her marrying some else! I will marry her. Will you help me, if needed?"

"I will, as much as I can and as long as I am not breaking any law. But what exactly is your plan?"

"I will let you know. Don't tell this to Mustafa and Gaurav. We have to keep my marriage plans a secret."

"Okay, I won't tell them, but how long will you be able to keep this secret?"

"Shalini has said that she can only hold out till Mains, and during this period she wants me to marry her."

"In the next three months? That's…"

"I want to marry her as soon as possible," he said and stood up.

He left my room; he seemed to have made up his mind. Love is blind and apparently hasty and impatient too.

I followed him to his room and said, "Are you going to elope? Where will you keep her after the marriage?"

"She will stay at home until the Mains. After that, she would tell her parents about our marriage. We will then discuss our options, depending upon how our parents react. Meanwhile, I must study like hell and become an IAS officer."

"I doubt if this plan will work."

"It is Shalini's plan."

Fearing it might make Balram angry if I doubted the plans his soon-to-be bride had made, I kept silent. *There's something fishy... something just not right with these plans. Anyway, why should I worry? It's their personal matter. As a good friend, I will help as long as my moral stance is not breached.*

Balram said, "You are going to be the witness from my side and Shalini will bring two more from her side."

Hearing this, a cold shiver ran down my spine. My mind was uneasy.

▼

I was clearly worried. Whenever I asked Balram about the secret wedding, he would always say, "Anytime! Be prepared for it and stay put. Don't leave Old Rajinder Nagar."

I was scared that some of their family members might end up beating me for being a witness. And the day came soon.

"Today is the day," said Balram, rubbing his hands together nervously. "I will give this jewellery to Shalini and then come pick you up." He showed me the jewellery: a mangalsutra, a nose ring, a set of earrings and anklets.

"This is a lot of gold. Where did you get the money for the jewellery?"

"I asked my dad for the money on the pretext of joining tuitions and test series for the Mains. Rest I borrowed from my old friends, gave them some excuses."

"So tell me, how are we doing this?" I was excited to hear the plan.

"First, Shalini and I will meet at a temple she has chosen in Noida. I will hand over the jewellery to her and check if the temple is suitable. She will go to her friend's house to get ready and return with her friends, who will witness the marriage from her side. I'll come and pick you up." Saying this, Balram left.

Within three hours, he was back. Excited to get married, he took a quick shower, dressed up in a new formal shirt, pants and leather shoes. We left for Noida in the Metro. "Hope it turns out all right. I just can't believe all this is happening!" he said, before getting into the Metro.

I couldn't believe it either, so I just smiled at him. Our journey from Karol Bagh to Noida City Centre was made in silence. We then took a rickshaw to an isolated temple near a desolate, under-construction building. I was uneasy as it is. The deserted location of the temple really gave me the creeps.

I saw that there was no one inside the temple as we approached it. Balram said, "Shalini said she would be here by 3 p.m. sharp. I hope she isn't wasting too much time getting dressed."

A priest emerged from the inner sanctum of the temple. As soon as he saw us, he went inside. We followed him in.

"Panditji, is everything ready?" asked Balram.

"Yes, beta. I'll just say my afternoon prayers. You kindly wait for ten minutes, and let's hope the girl reaches soon too," Panditji said, lighting a small earthenware lamp in front of Shivji's idol.

We occupied the bench on the sidewalk right in front of the temple. Twenty minutes into the waiting, there was still no sign of the bride.

Balram tried calling her, but there was no response. "She must be in the Metro. Her number says out of coverage area."

"Where does your *soon-to-be-bride* stay?" I asked.

"She stays somewhere in Ghaziabad. I don't remember exactly where. And you stop calling her my *soon-to-be-bride*. You can call her Shalini," replied Balram, sounding peeved and nervous.

In a flurry of dust, an old Tata Sumo drove up and screeched to a halt before us. A few inches more and it would have mangled us to a pulp. Six men in their late twenties got down from the vehicle with hockey sticks and baseball bats. Before we realized what was happening, one of them started shouting.

"Who is Balram here?" he yelled. He was dressed in ripped jeans, black shirt, shiny golden shoes and had golden streaks in his hair.

Balram stood up and anxiously said, "It's me. What's the matter?"

"So, you are Balram. You want to marry her, huh?"

He caught hold of Balram by his collar and shook him, holding a hockey stick in the other hand. I tried to interfere, but there was a heavy blow on my collarbone and then on my knee. I fell on the ground but was conscious. I saw two men holding Balram while the golden hair guy began hitting his stomach, thigh and then on his face with the hockey stick.

"You want to marry her? Just stay away from her!" he shouted like a madman.

Balram's face was bleeding. I tried to get up and help Balram, but two guys caught me by my shoulder and held me back. I tried to free myself from their grip, but I just couldn't, because of the pain in my knee.

"We love each other and want to marry. Who are you to interfere?" Balram spoke up.

"I am her boyfriend! She loves me. If I see you trying to contact her again…" said the man, and he struck Balram again on the face with the hockey stick.

In a semi-conscious state, Balram started babbling something as the blood started oozing out of his mouth. The man was abusing Balram with choicest of foul words while he chanted Shalini's name. The gang started laughing. "Her name is not Shalini."

"I want to talk to Shalini, my Shalini," said Balram, almost fainting.

"Oh, so you want to talk to Shalini? Wait, I will call her," he said and called up someone on the mobile. He placed the phone on Balram's ear.

I could see Balram saying something into the mobile phone and then he was quietly listening.

"You lying bitch," he shouted into the mobile. The guy slapped Balram so hard that he fell unconscious to the ground.

Then the man came to me and said, "Tell your friend never to contact her again. If he does, he knows what will happen. And don't you try contacting the police." I felt a heavy blow on my head from behind and that was the last thing I remembered.

When I regained consciousness, I looked at my phone, it was 5:30 p.m. The temple doors were closed, and Panditji was nowhere to be seen. *He must have been hand-in-glove with those men who beat us up... That's why he didn't interfere or call the police when we were being bashed up!*

Balram was lying unconscious. I was relieved to see that he was still breathing. He was bleeding badly. I tried waking him up, but to no avail. I somehow managed to pick him up and get him to rest against the bench and then I went in search of water. After walking for 800-meters or so, I found a tapri from where I bought water pouches. I poured some water from the pouch on Balram's face and head. He regained consciousness after some time, but he was still bewildered by the turn of events. We both sat there on the bench, clueless and exhausted with pain.

Balram started crying, holding onto me, his bleeding face on my shoulder. "Her name is not Shalini Meena, she never stayed in Ghaziabad and she was never preparing for UPSC," he said. He started sobbing hard.

I put my arm around his shoulder. "Let's contact the police or tell your father about this. He will surely find these goons."

"No way are we contacting police or my father!" he said alarmed. "If we do so, she will press rape charges against me and put me behind bars. Worse, it will also affect my dad's clean image in front of the public and hamper his political career." Balram was baffled by what had happened. He just wasn't ready to come to terms with the reality that his first love was actually just an elaborate con.

"Why did I accept her demand for the jewellery? Why couldn't I see through her intentions?" he said with gritted teeth, justifiably angry with himself.

"She asked for the jewellery herself? I thought you were giving it of your own accord!"

"No, I didn't. I obviously didn't have the money to buy it. It was she who asked me for it. She said that gold was considered auspicious and wished to wear it on our wedding day."

"Don't blame yourself now. You were in love."

Somehow we made our way back to Old Rajinder Nagar that night. But we never shared this incident with anyone, not even Gaurav and Mustafa.

I was able to hide my sore shoulders and knees, but Balram had to cook up a story about how he was robbed and beaten up late last night in a narrow deserted lane behind by unknown men whose faces he couldn't see properly in the dark.

Balram was never the same after the incident. He would keep himself locked in his room. He avoided my eyes whenever I spoke to him. It was only Mustafa who would study with me thereafter, but that was also short-lived.

25

The Casualties

Within a fortnight of the event that had completely shattered Balram, the UPSC Civil Service Prelims 2012 results were declared. Balram cleared, but Mustafa did not, neither did Sakshi or Indu. Ankit, Abhijeet, Rohini and I cleared. I wasn't surprised to hear that Rajiv Ranjan Jha had also cleared the Prelims.

Here was another chance to redeem myself, but the past memories of failure, where I had given my best shot, were fresh. I soldiered on as much as I could, but without the zeal, enthusiasm and efficiency I had earlier.

Mustafa left Old Rajinder Nagar without a goodbye. The people who knew him told me that he didn't want to keep in touch with any of us because it reminded him of his failure. Later, some mutual acquaintances informed us that he had joined his father's business. He visited Delhi from time to time because of the proceeding of the compensation court case. That's the last I heard of him. Just like that, he vanished from my life as if he was never there.

The positive result in Prelims did little to raise Balram's spirits. He looked weak, fragile and had lost weight. One day he came to my room in his unkempt beard and eyes red with lack of sleep.

"I am going home. I miss my parents, especially my mother," he announced.

"Will you study for Mains from home?"

"I am going to skip this attempt. I am not going to appear for the Mains this year," he said. He couldn't look into my eyes.

I just kept looking at him for a few seconds in silence.

"Why are you wasting this attempt? You have studied so much; why not just write the exam. Skipping this attempt would mean another two years for clearing this exam or even longer if you don't clear next time too."

"I am not in the right frame of mind. I just can't get her out of my head. I hear her voice all the time. I just can't focus; just can't... stop thinking about her."

After a few moments of silence, he continued. "I'll be back, but as of now, I need to recover and home is the best place to do it. I wanted to leave right after the incident, but the bruises on my face and the black eye were quite visible. If my father had seen it, he would have wormed the reason out of me."

By the end of August, Balram had vacated the room, although he still continued to rent it.

I missed Mustafa's Urdu couplets and his delicious cooking and Balram's simplicity.

I was once again back in Gaurav's room for studying. Watching him prepare for his medical entrance would motivate me to study too, I thought.

▼

One night, Ankit made a surprise visit to my room. It had been more than two months since I had met him. After the exam results, when Sakshi flunked, matters seemed to have taken a turn for the worst for him.

"What happened, dude? Is everything all right?" I asked.

"I am sorry. I know I am disturbing you. But you are the only person I can think of turning to whenever I have a problem."

"Is it related to Sakshi?"

He nodded.

"What happened now?"

"You know she flunked in the Prelims again and her parents are pushing her to get married."

"Well then, that's good. What's the problem? Marry her."

"I would, if her parents agreed."

"And why wouldn't they agree?"

"Because I belong to a lower caste than her."

"But you are not SC/ST or OBC. You belong to the general category."

"Yes, but still in the fucking caste hierarchy of our Hindu caste system, my caste ranks lower than hers."

"Which caste do you belong to man?"

"I am a Vaishya and she is a Kshatriya."

"But in history, Gupta dynasty ruled over India. Your surname is Gupta. I thought even you were Kshatriya."

"Guptas are Baniyas, which means traders."

"So how come they ruled India if they were traders? I thought only Kshatriya could be kings and Brahmin could be priests?"

"Why the fuck are we talking about Gupta dynasty and kings and priests? I am losing my girl and you are interested in digging out the history of our country."

"I am sorry; I just got a bit confused. Ask Sakshi to go tell her parents about you and your family background. You hail from a bureaucratic family like hers. I think her parents will understand."

"She tried telling her parents about me, but the moment she said she was in love with someone outside her caste, her father strictly told her that if she marries someone outside the community, he would leave the house. When she persisted and requested that they meet me, her mother said that she will commit suicide if Sakshi marries outside the community."

With that, to my horror, Ankit burst into sobs. I had never imagined that caste could be a problem even in such well-educated families. *Sakshi's father is an IPS officer, for god's sake! He should know better.*

"She was home when her parents started blackmailing her emotionally into marrying someone else. She started distancing herself from me after that. She said we should be friends as there is no future," Ankit said, breaking into my thoughts.

"Do you guys still talk to each other?"

"Yes, we do, and for appearance's sake we are in a relationship, but it's kind of one-sided. I begged her to stay till the Mains. I need her support, but I know she no longer feels involved."

"The fact that she has agreed to stay in the relationship shows that she cares. I think the best option for you is to give it time and hold on to her the way she wants. Focus on your Mains. God willing, you will become an IAS with AIR below 10 and her dad might reconsider."

"Well that's exactly what the plan is, but there is the ever-present fear. What if she gets married before I can clear this treacherous exam?"

"I can understand, but what other option do you have?"

Helplessly, he nodded and agreed with me. We drank Old Monk all night. Before I was up in the morning, Ankit was gone.

26

Guwahati Chronicles

It was September already. The Mains exam was thirty-five days away, as was my first visit to the beautiful North-eastern India. The farthest east I had ever been was Kolkata. I waited eagerly for my Guwahati visit.

I hoped Abhijeet's strategy worked. I was not sure if I would be able to survive another failure in Civil Service exams. I wondered if Ankit would be able to survive it.

▼

Almost every night in the last month before the exam, I had spent counselling Ankit. After 10 p.m. each evening, we devoted an hour to analysing what Sakshi had said, and the hidden meaning in it, if any. I didn't mind. All day, I talked to no one except the maid and Gaurav. If it weren't for Ankit, I would have been talking to the walls.

As the Mains exam date drew closer, Ankit told me that Sakshi had started sending feelers to him. There could be a way of postponing her marriage. She had told her parents that if they allowed her to write one last attempt of UPSC Civil service exam, then she would wholeheartedly submit to their desire of marrying the man of their choice.

Knowing that he had one last chance to make it into IAS, and marrying the love of his life, raised Ankit's hopes. Our conversations in the dark hours turned from those of depression and hopelessness to hope and optimism.

Ankit was very excited about this chance offered by Sakshi. But with all this hope also came anxiety. Sometimes I felt it would have been better if Sakshi hadn't given him any hope, but other times I felt this slow poison might turn out to be the cure for Ankit.

▼

Finally it was time for the Mains. While the others had to travel an hour or so for their centre, I had to catch a flight. And that I did.

I landed at Guwahati in the afternoon; it looked beautiful from above. It was an expanse of lush greenery. The scars of the recent floods were clearly visible as we approached the airport. There was heavy security at the airport because of the recent ethnic-religious clashes.

I collected my luggage and was about to exit the airport building when a woman officer belonging to CISF asked me to show my flight ticket. I put my hands in my pocket to bring out the ticket but it was not there. I had misplaced it. I searched in all the other pockets. The lady CISF officer stared at me suspiciously. I felt helpless and must surely have looked it.

I wanted to show her the e-Ticket in my mail but my mobile battery had discharged. She asked me for my ID and I produced my driving license. In the driving license, I had a 2005 photo, in which I looked relatively younger. I was older now and sported a full beard and long curly hair. The mismatch didn't help.

"From where did you board the flight and what is the purpose of your visit to Guwahati?" the lady officer asked.

"I have come to appear for an exam."

"Which exam?"

"UPSC Civil Services Mains exam."

"Why would you come to Guwahati from Delhi for UPSC civil service exam? Aren't there any centres in Delhi?"

"Yes, but I wanted to give it from outside Delhi."

"Why?"

"Because someone told me one gets good marks in UPSC Civil Service exam if one appears from Guwahati." Even to me, it sounded horribly stupid. I wished the earth would swallow me up. The officer's lip curled up in a sneer.

The officer noted my luggage tags. She took me to the Indigo counter to cross-check if there was anyone travelling by my name. Thankfully the man at Air Indigo desk confirmed my presence in the flight. She told me I was free to go and I heaved a sigh of relief.

I was about to leave the counter when I heard her voice again. "Excuse me, all the very best for the Mains. I gave all my UPSC Civil Service attempts from Guwahati but I could never clear the Mains. Somehow I managed to clear the Central Armed Police Force exam (CAPF) and landed a job in CISF."

I looked at her for a few seconds with a smile on my face. I didn't know what to say, but just thanked her for her wishes and left. What a welcome to Guwahati!

▼

After strenuous objection to my going to Guwahati, my dad had made my staying arrangements at a lodge. It was an hour's drive through the scenic verdant roads from the Lokpriya Gopinath Bordoloi Airport to the lodge. I could see the mountains all around me. The place had a sleepy feel to it. It started to drizzle again by the time we reached the lodge, a three-storied building. At the counter, I saw no one, but behind the counter was a door which led to another room. An old man sat there, reading a newspaper.

"Excuse me, sir," I called. In slow motion, a face peered out from behind the newspaper. He got up from his netted bamboo chair cushioned with a pillow and came to the counter.

"Sir, I have a room reservation here."

The old man put up his glasses and started flipping through the pages of his register. I noticed that he didn't look at me even once. His eyes were always lowered and he didn't say a word to me.

"May I have your ID card?" he finally said, still staring down at the register.

Then he matched the name on my ID with the one on his register. "Please sign here." He pointed on the page with his finger. "204 is your room number."

"Do we get Red Bull energy drink here?" I asked him.

"Yes, there are alcohol shops around, but you cannot drink in the room."

I laughed. "Why would I drink alcohol and give my exam?"

"How do I know? Alcohol might be your source of energy?" I couldn't stop laughing. The old man did have a sense of humour.

"Do you have a fridge here?"

"Yes, there is one in the kitchen but you can't keep alcohol in it."

Without bothering to explain to him that I didn't want the fridge to store alcohol but Red Bull, I asked him, "Do you have geysers for hot water in the room?"

"No, not in the room, but we can provide you with warm water for ten rupees per bucket."

I completed the formalities at the reception desk. I was going to be an occupant of the lodge for fifteen days – 2nd to 16th October.

"Bulbul," yelled the old man, obviously calling someone. After a pause, he called again.

"Bulbul! Bulbul! Ah, there you are! Please show this gentleman his room and help him with his luggage."

A boy of twelve had emerged from a door that led towards the staircase. He had a very prominent scar over his right eye. He was weakly built and had a dark complexion. Without saying a word, he picked up my bag, heavy for a boy of his age and built. He struggled with the bag but didn't complain. I asked the boy to leave it and looked at the old man. But he had retreated to his room behind the reception counter. The boy somehow managed to carry the bag with all his might to the second floor. I tipped him fifty rupees. His face broke into a huge grin. Eyes shining, he took the money.

"Babuji, if you have any work like cleaning the room, washing your clothes, polishing your shoes or getting anything from the market, call me."

I smiled and nodded before closing the door. The place was quiet, even though the window opened right outside over the road. There was an attached washroom, and a small cupboard to keep clothes. I was comfortable.

I lit a cigarette as I stood watching out of the window. I could see shops and some government office, which looked deserted. Behind it all, I could see the mountains on the horizon.

I was tired but wasn't feeling sleepy so I decided to check out my examination centre, an engineering college by the name of Assam Engineering Institute, which according to Google map was barely a kilometre away.

I was happy to have found Red Bull at the liquor store, but it was the sugar-free one, which tasted like cough syrup.

That day I had lunch at 4 p.m. in the small make-shift restaurant made of bamboo and plastic next to my lodge. I was surprised to see Bulbul working there too, serving food to the customers. He looked at me and smiled. The eating place was small and you had to share the table with a stranger.

"What would you like to have, Babuji?" Bulbul asked me.

"What do you get here? Can I see the menu?"

"There is no menu. You only get veg, chicken and maccha (fish) thali, babumoshai," said the owner of the restaurant, coming out from behind the curtain used to conceal the kitchen.

I ordered a fish thali. The fish thali had *rohu* fish, baingan bhajha, fried potatoes, yellow dal, two rotis and unlimited rice. This meal cost me just fifty rupees and the food was palatable. In the evening, I turned up again for dinner and was again greeted by the two familiar faces and an empty restaurant.

The cook was in his 60s, and he and Bulbul were the only two people working at the place. The man would cook and Bulbul would serve and wash the utensils later, and after that, would also work at the lodge. I felt sorry for Bulbul. Barely twelve years old and so much work!

I lay on my bed thinking about Bulbul. With my room lights switched off and only the streetlights making shadows of the passing cars on the wall in front of me, my bed began shaking. Earthquake!

I ran out of my room into an empty corridor. Were they in such a deep sleep that they failed to experience it? When I reached the ground floor, I saw Bulbul relaxing on the sofa. He lay watching cartoon network in the dim light.

"What happened, Babuji?" he asked.

"There was an earthquake, so I ran down. Didn't you experience it?"

"It's normal here. Such tremors happen every now and then. We are accustomed to them. Even you will get used to it, don't worry," said Bulbul casually.

His casual words did nothing to relieve my anxiety and fear. I couldn't sleep until 3 a.m., waiting to feel the tremors again. There were two more shocks but I didn't run, putting my faith in Bulbul's assurance that such tremors were normal and would not bring the lodge down.

27

Bulbul

Only two days were left for my first paper of General Studies. I got down to studying whatever I could from the parts I had marked and highlighted in the different books. It was impossible to revise and I knew this. But I had two days to go before the exam. I studied while repeating to myself every now and then, "Look, this is going to be the final attempt and you are going to get selected."

Every morning Bulbul came to my room with a bucket of hot water for my bath and to clean the room and toilet. I paid him ten rupees for the hot water and an additional twenty rupees for reasons of sympathy. He would smile and hop away. In the afternoon and late evening, I would meet him at the restaurant.

My exams began. The Mains GS Paper-I and II were not only analytical but also voluminous, needing me to write reams! The questions were dynamic. Such unseen questions, I was at my wit's end, predicting the UPSC's mood. It was easier to gauging the mood of a woman than that of UPSC!

All I remember is that I was successful in my mission of attempting almost all of the questions asked in the General Studies paper, even if that meant writing fiction. I was a bit scared of the Hindi paper, but somehow managed to attempt it with much satisfaction. I didn't bother thinking much about how my English and Essay paper fared.

Here I was, halfway between my exams. I had a seven-day break before my Psychology and Philosophy optional papers, which were on consecutive days.

It was 8th October and I was woken up by a knock on my door. I had slept pretty late the night before. It was Bulbul. "Babuji I had come in the morning with hot water, but you didn't open the door."

"I was sleeping," I said.

Bulbul started cleaning the room. I lit a cigarette noting how Bulbul was cleaning the room. He was too young to have the scar he had on his face. One day when he was cleaning the room, my sympathy for Bulbul intensified my curiosity to talk to him about his life.

I asked him, "What is your real name, Bulbul?"

"Aminul Islam, Babuji."

"Why do they call you Bulbul?"

"My dad named me after a cricketer. He was a big fan of cricket."

I had never heard about this cricketer before. A Google search showed Aminul Islam Bulbul was a Bangladeshi cricketer. Why would an Indian name his son after some obscure Bangladeshi cricketer, I wondered?

"Where does your father work?"

"Very far away, Babuji. I don't know the name of the place but Das Sahib says he will come soon to take me."

Ah! The lodge owner was Mr Das!

"How did you get the scar on your forehead?"

"I don't remember how, Babuji. One day I woke up and it was there."

"Do you go to school?"

"I wish to, but I am very poor. My father will bring lots of money when he returns from the far-off place where he works. Then I will join a good school. Till then, I am also saving money."

"Which is your native place?"

"I don't know the name, but I remember the place. It wasn't a big city like this, only a small village."

The way he answered my questions made me more curious about Bulbul's past. I didn't ask him any more questions that day since I had an exam to give. I gave him a hundred rupee note that day; the smile on his face was worth it.

▼

That night after dinner, I watched the highlights of the T20 World Cup finals between West Indies and Sri Lanka. West Indies were the new champions. In 2011, India had won the World Cup and I failed in passing my exams. This year, India failed to qualify for the semi-finals, and I wondered if I would clear the Civils this year? I don't know how I ended up drawing such conclusions, but I tried to read signs which somehow indicated that I was going to succeed in this exam.

"We defeated Pakistan in the league matches and still Pakistan managed to qualify for the semi-finals. We couldn't because of our bad net run rate. Bloody Pakistanis!" said Mr Das, sitting on the chair behind the reception desk.

"That was our bad luck, uncle," I replied. To be frank, I hadn't been following this year's T20 World Cup.

"We defeated Pakistan. That is as good as winning the T20 World Cup for me. They would never be able to defeat us in a World Cup or in a war. Look how we defeated them in the 1971 war and created Bangladesh. They had committed rampant butchery and rape in Bangladesh! We still suffer from the spill-over effects of that war," said Mr Das, sipping from a steel glass.

Mr Das's reference to the Bangladesh war had caught my attention. I wondered how the topic had changed from cricket to war. Hatred does this; it drags our attention to the most unpleasant memories. The manner in which he was talking made me realize that Mr Das was drunk.

"Look, so many people died in the ethnic communal clashes in Kokrajhar district. Countless refugees could never return to Bangladesh after the 1971 war. For a while, they thought they could return peacefully, but after the assassination of Sheikh Mujibur Rahman, the new government refused to accept their own people as citizens of their country.

"Bulbul's father was one such person. I found his sixteen-year-old father at Guwahati railway station. Those days I worked for Indian Railways. The sudden death of my mother, father and elder brother in a car accident compelled me to quit the job. I returned to Kokrajhar to look after our small family business consisting of shops and two lodges. Feeling sorry for Bulbul's father, I took him with me to Kokrajhar.

"He was an honest and hardworking boy. With time he turned into a loyal servant and friend. My shops in Kokrajhar were looked after by Bulbul's father. I came down to Guwahati to look after the lodge here. I could not bear to stay in Kokrajhar. It reminded me of my parents and elder brother and filled me with sadness. They were on the way from Kokrajhar to Guwahati to meet me when they met with that fatal accident."

I heard Mr Das sobbing. I walked up to him and put my hand on his old and weary shoulder as he sat on the chair behind the reception. It was already 11 p.m. Bulbul had not come back from the restaurant yet. Otherwise, he too would have been sitting on the sofa, watching cartoon network before going to sleep.

Meanwhile, Mr Das continued in a heavy, choked voice filled with sadness. "Bulbul's father and I had both lost our families. It created a bond between us. We only had each other. He was someone I could rely on as a friend for support. For forty years he worked for me, looking after my shops where he stayed with his wife and son.

"One fine day, in the last week of July, I received a call from my neighbours in Kokrajhar about the rioting, looting and burning of my shop. I rushed there, only to find my shops turned to cinder. Bulbul and his parents were missing. I rushed to the nearest hospital to check if they were admitted there. It was much worse. At the hospital, I found the half-burnt bodies of Bulbul's father and mother. The doctor informed me of a kid who was being treated for injuries and still unconscious for the past two days and whose parents' identity was still unknown.

"And there lay little Bulbul. I found him as an orphan, just like I had found his dad as an orphan forty years ago. After a few days, he regained consciousness, but he couldn't remember much except a little about his father. I told him that his father had gone with his mother to a far off place to work and make money. Until they returned, Bulbul could stay with me and help me with my lodge.

"I am sixty-five years old now and I don't know how long I'll live. I barely make a living out of this lodge. All my shops back in Kokrajhar have been turned to ashes. I have to look after Bulbul. Just like his father, Bulbul is a hard-working boy. He helps me in my lodge and also at the restaurant next to the lodge. With whatever savings I have, I wish to send him to school from next year. God bless the boy!"

Mr Das got up from his chair and retired to his room behind the reception. Tears had welled up in my eyes. I was about to go upstairs when I saw Bulbul sitting on the steps, playing snakes and ladders on a Nokia 3310 mobile phone. I thought those phones had become extinct.

"When did you come back from the restaurant?"

"Twenty minutes ago, Babuji. I saw Das Sahib and you talking and watching the match so thought of not interrupting your discussion."

"You can watch the cartoons now. Goodnight, Bulbul."

▼

My stay in Guwahati crept slowly away, one day at a time. I prayed fervently for Bulbul's future and helped him in whatever way I could. Whenever I tipped him now, I did not see the former innocent smile, oozing happiness. He just thanked me and left with a dull face.

Soon it was time for the exam for optional subjects. It was going to be a very draining experience since I had back-to-back exams in Psychology and Philosophy. The sleeping pills helped me to at least get refreshing sleep. My Psychology paper wasn't as I expected. There were too many questions of statistics in Paper-I, which I had not revised. I just managed to write something as I did for my General Studies paper.

Philosophy was also nothing exceptional, except that I completed the paper. I was devoting precious years of my life preparing for an exam I didn't have a clue about. I had no idea whether I was on the right path, nor if I did well in the exam. I just submitted myself to my destiny.

Finally, the exam was over! I was to leave the very next day. I took my sleeping pills for one last time so I could be up early. I had to leave for the airport by 9 a.m. But despite the sleeping pill, I couldn't sleep. My muscles were aching because of continuous writing for twelve hours in two days. My fingers had swollen. My arms refused to bend; the side-effect of Red Bull overdose. I had been consuming three Red Bulls a day for the past two days. I needed to sleep to rest my muscles, but the end of exams took away the pressure suddenly and this newfound freedom, although it would be short-lived, took away all the anxiety and tension.

I had asked Bulbul to wake me up in case I was still sleepy. He woke me up at seven in the morning, bringing along the bucket of hot water. I was ready by 8:30 a.m. waiting at the reception for the cab. Bulbul was sitting right beside me, having helped me with bringing down the luggage from my room. Mr Das was also up and I had to make the payment for my stay.

"Bulbul, make some Lal chai for Babuji and me," said Mr Das as he started to count the money I paid him and made a receipt.

I sat on the sofa again and after some time, Bulbul brought the Lal chai. Then Mr Das sat next to me, sipping on his Lal chai. "Hope you had a pleasant stay here in my lodge without any problem?" he asked.

"Yes, Mr Das, it was a pleasant stay. You and Bulbul took excellent care of me."

"I am so happy to hear this. Kindly do suggest my lodge to your friends if they intend to come to Chandmari for any purpose. Please do visit us again."

"I would for sure, Mr Das," I said with a smile as Bulbul helped me put my luggage in the cab. Before getting into the car, I gave Bulbul a tight hug. I also gave him two thousand rupees. He took it, but I still couldn't manage to get that smile back on his face.

"Do look after Mr Das. He is old and needs you. Also, work hard and save money," I told him.

"There is no point saving money, Babuji," he replied.

"Why, Bulbul?"

"I will never be able to save enough to afford my education. And as you know, my father is never going to come back." Tears started rolling down his cheeks and he ran inside. I followed Bulbul inside the lodge, but I couldn't find him. Mr Das had retracted back to his room behind the reception desk. I had no option but to leave. I had a flight to catch and the airport was far off.

On my way to the airport, I promised myself that if ever I cleared this exam, I would come back to this lodge again to meet Mr Das and Bulbul and try my best to help Bulbul get proper education and a good life.

The flight back to Delhi from Guwahati and the familiar distant sight of mountains from the airplane window reminded me that I too had a mountain to climb and the name of my mountain was UPSC, as treacherous and as unpredictable to climb as Mount Everest.

28

British Council

I was back from Guwahati with memories of Mr Das and Bulbul alive and lingering. It was a long wait for the Mains result to be declared. More than four months. I had to keep myself busy. The last week of October and all of November was spent watching the new season of *Game of Thrones*, *How I Met Your Mother*, *The Big Bang Theory* and an endless stream of movies. When I was bored of it all, I roamed around Delhi with Ankit and Sakshi.

Ankit was planning to holiday in Australia at his uncle's place and he was supposed to leave on 1st December. Sakshi was also planning a two-month-long vacation with her parents in London. She would be visiting her older brother. She planned to leave on the third Sunday of December. Ankit had his suspicions regarding Sakshi's visit to London and wasn't happy with it.

"I won't get to see Sakshi for two months. Why is she going to stay in London for two months?" said Ankit, a desperate lover complaining about the impending absence of his beloved.

"I know you are going to miss her, but even you are going to Australia. I am sure your mind will be occupied with *firang* beauties," I said, in a lighter vein.

"My Sakshi is more beautiful than any *firang* girl! I am going to Australia for only for ten days. She won't be able to talk much when in London, as she will be under the nose of her strict father. I get a bad feeling that they are going to London for Sakshi to meet some suitable guy arranged for her by the family."

I didn't say much. It was obvious that such fears would occupy Ankit's mind. "Did you ask her?" I asked.

"I did and we even fought over this. She is denying it, but I know."

"Relax, Ankit! If she is saying so, then that must be the case."

So here was December knocking at my door and I was thoroughly bored with life. People said it was better to start preparing for the interview. I did try to study for my interview by going through biodata form, but within days I gave up on the idea, just like last time. I thought it was way too early to prepare for the interview and the fact that deep down inside my heart I knew I was clueless how I had done in the exam. Going by last years' experience, I had zero confidence in clearing it.

So what should I do with my time? There were still three months to go. Ankit and Sakshi had left for their respective vacations and Gaurav was preparing for his medical entrance exams, which were in December and January. Balram had not returned to his room and Rajiv Ranjan Jha continued to live his reclusive, dark life.

It was Abhijeet who helped me to kill my boredom by giving me some useful advice when I met him on a December morning.

"So what are you up to?" asked Abhijeet.

"TV serials, movies and sleep."

"Not studying for the interview? Are you expecting a call?"

"I am clueless. What about you?"

"Yes, I am expecting to clear. This year the papers went far better than last year, so I am very hopeful. Rest its destiny."

"Can you suggest something interesting for me to do?"

"Why don't you do something related to poetry? Rohini told me you are a good poet. She has read some of the work you shared with Indu."

It felt good whenever people praised my poems. That's one thing that got me excited. I so wished they had poetry as a subject in UPSC. "Thank you. I do write poems every now and then, but it's not a full-time affair."

"You only write poems, right? Ever thought of writing a novel?" asked Abhijeet.

"Yes, I do plan to get into prose writing."

"Perfect. Then I think I do have the perfect cure for you to pass your time constructively."

"And what cure would be that?"

"Have you heard about the British Council? They have a Creative Writing class. My sister had joined last year and she said it's beneficial for newbie writers. Also, I remember you got only 40 marks in the Essay paper last time, right?"

"Yes, and I couldn't clear the Mains by five marks," I said remorsefully.

"Then I think it will help you to write and present your essay more creatively and help you score good marks. You can mention the certificate in the UPSC interview too," said a smiling Abhijeet. I knew what that smile meant.

And so, there I was at the British Council. After a preliminary exam to check my level of understanding of English and an interview, they found me fit to apply for the Creative Writing course, which I did. My classes were to start in the first week of January, fifteen days away.

Thank god, Ankit was back from his ten-day visit to Australia! Each day crawled by like a burden. I just couldn't make sense of my existence except that I was waiting to clear an exam. I wondered what revolution I would bring after clearing it. All you heard about Civil

Service at the Old Rajinder Nagar chai tapri was the amount of money you could make by becoming an IAS officer. Time and again, I argued with myself about my real purpose of giving the exam and I found none!

"Don't worry, Civil Serpentji, once you clear the exam, you will know why you gave it. It's just failure that is making you say sad things about it. I think you should first clear it and then criticize, if at all. Then people might appreciate your criticism. Otherwise, they will think it's a case of sour grapes," said Gaurav, when I went to his room to speak about my boredom and this long wait. I realized Gaurav was right.

This conversation was not headed the way I wanted it to. My mobile began to ring and gave me the excuse to leave Gaurav's room. As I entered my room, Sakshi's angelic voice greeted me on the phone. She said, "Would you mind joining Ankit and me for a movie? I am leaving for London, so thought we should all catch up."

"Yes, sure. When should we meet?"

"Ankit will pick you up in an hour, he told me. Please coordinate with him."

In an hour, as usual, Ankit picked me up from Gol Chakkar.

"Which movie are we going to?" I asked him.

"She wants to watch *Life of Pi*. I wanted to see some action movie, but there is no action movie running at present," said Ankit.

Ankit loved watching action movies, no matter how boring the movie was. I think he had a lot of suppressed feelings and frustrations, the gratification of which he achieved by vicarious reinforcement. If UPSC had been a person, all the violence he saw in action movies, he'd have unleashed upon it.

"So which movie hall are we going to?" I asked.

"PVR Select City Walk, Saket. Sakshi will be waiting for us at the movie hall with tickets."

On the cold evening of 16th December 2012, we met Sakshi at the mall. She was wearing a lovely white skirt, a long overcoat paired with boots. God knows from where she had bought the mesmerizing perfume. She was a picture of perfection and that smile of hers made my heart skip a beat. How are you supposed to concentrate on the movie when you have such a beautiful lady by your side? Looking at Sakshi, I could understand Ankit's fear of losing her. Sakshi was probably the only thing that Ankit possessed that made me jealous of him.

After the movie, we had dinner at Geoffrey's. This farewell meeting with Sakshi turned out to be an actual farewell to Sakshi at least for me, if not for Ankit.

I remember the night of 16th December 2012 because that was the last time I ever met Sakshi, although we continued to speak on the phone. The date was unforgettable for all Indians. Like them, I will never forget the night because it shook the conscience of the whole nation. It was the night a young girl had watched the same movie, in the same movie-hall. She had gone home with her friend. In the bus, they were brutally attacked. She was raped and brutalized in a way that defied description. She was thrown out of the moving bus, still fighting for her life. She lay by the side of the road like a crumpled paper bag until she was rushed to the hospital.

Her name was Nirbhaya.

29

The Accident

As the brutal details of Nirbhaya's rape started pouring in, the outraged nation exploded with protests at India Gate and Raisina Hill.

India was incensed with the case and with the process of law that was both inefficient and slow in punishing the criminals. There were protests not only in India but the world over. Many restaurants, clubs and pubs declared a moratorium on New Year celebrations that year. The usually sleepy Old Rajinder Nagar too was abuzz. People were high on sentiment, which was natural. Discussions at lowly chai tapris and posh cafes covered the social, cultural, psychological and legal perspectives into account.

Many aspirants prophesied that questions relating to the incident could be expected next year. Much of the discussion also revolved around the fact that one of the perpetrators of the crime was juvenile and whether he should be hanged or not. Questions on Juvenile Justice Act could also be expected. The juvenile was reportedly the most barbaric of the five people involved in the rape, but according to the present Indian law, he would be set free in just three years because he was below the legal age to stand trial as an adult. The last ten days of the year slid past in the shadow of this horror.

Even on the morning of 31st December, when Abhijeet called me to wish Happy New Year in advance, the pleasantries were followed by the discussion about the injustice women face.

"Who do you think is to be blamed for rape and all our other social problems?" asked Abhijeet.

"The society, who else? Our culture frowns upon premarital sex, which in turn creates the sexually suppressed and frustrated society of India, where sex crimes are higher than the West. We have to consider serious punishments for such crimes."

"Yes, but there should not be knee-jerk reactions. Laws should be made strict, but it should not be on the premise that all men are rapists. Sometimes women file rape cases against men on malafide grounds. I don't know how to correctly achieve balanced and just. That is for the legal fraternity to decide, but all I can say is that we as a society should change our mindset. We have to rise above gender, caste and religious divide not only during the time of crisis but also when there is no crisis. Only then can this country become a better place to live."

"Wish it was as easy as you have said," I told him.

"I know it is easier said than done, but I still feel that if we try it might work. I don't know if we will see the India of our dreams in our life, but we will surely be a bridge the next generation can use to reach that point. ," Abhijeet said philosophically.

"I agree, dude."

"Anyway, I am leaving for Jaipur in the evening. Going home for the New Year. Catch up with you when I return. Happy New Year once again."

"Happy New Year to you too."

▼

Little did I know the first day of the New Year would turn out to be the way it did. It was afternoon and I was still battling last night's hangover. I was about to crash in for an afternoon siesta when Rohini called up.

"Hello, are you there?" Rohini voice was tearful.

"Hey, what happened?"

"Abhijeet met with an accident. He is no more."

I was jolted out of my hangover. What awful news! I was stunned, my brain frozen, my vocal cords jammed.

First Manish and then Abhijeet... are you happy now? How could you allow such a brutal thing to happen? All part of your sinister plan, isn't it? Aren't you happy with the usual grief and frustrations you dump on us? A guy like Abhijeet did not deserve such fate! It took me a few minutes to realize that I was talking to the Almighty.

Abhijeet had been travelling to Jaipur with his family. His parents and sister were sitting at the rear of the car, and he was sitting in front. His driver suffered a heart attack while driving and died instantly, leaving the car out of control. The car crashed into the truck coming towards them. It was a head-on collision. His parents and sister survived, but he died on the spot. Later, as fate would have it, we learned that Abhijeet had cleared the Mains that year.

It was a cruel irony. God's sense of timing sucked.

30

Almost Married

It was the first day of my Creative Writing class at the British Council. All I could think of was Abhijeet's premature death. He was the one who suggested these classes, after all. *Abhijeet was just twenty-four when he died. He spent four years of his life preparing for an exam so he could live a better life and serve the country and this dream just vaporized. No one can understand the games god plays with us humans!*

A diverse crowd of twenty people were seated in the class being held on the second floor. People were as young as sixteen to as old as seventy. The teacher, Bharat, was a guy in his 20s, though his beard made him look older. The class time was from 4:30 p.m. to 6:30 p.m. In the class, women slightly outnumbered men. Most of them were college girls studying English literature at Delhi University. The first day was spent in discussing our dreams and expectations from the class, and introductions. There were some ice-breaking exercises for us to become acquainted.

By the end of the class, we were given our identity cards. There would be two classes of two hours each per week, on Monday and Thursday—a total of sixteen classes in two months. If you were absent for more than two classes, you would not get the certificate. My eyes scanned the participants and stopped on one. Her name was Isha Bagga.

▼

My friendship with Isha Bagga kept my mind from straying into the dark lanes of loneliness. It started with being in the same group for the assignment in class at British Council to messaging on WhatsApp for assignment discussions. As the days passed, our friendship grew. One day Isha asked me out for lunch. She thought since I have studied psychology, I'll be able to help her with a character sketch she had been working on. This was the first time any girl had asked me out, and although it didn't sound like a date, I hoped I could count it as one because I had started falling for her.

It was somewhere in the third week of January, a pleasant winter afternoon in Delhi had brought us to Café Coast in Hauz Khas. "It's hard to give up everything and become a writer." Isha sipped her caramello, looked at me and then stared out of the window. *She looks beautiful, her lips seem so soft.* "It's been two years since I gave up my job. Been one year since I decided not to join ISB Hyderabad," she continued bringing me out of my reverie.

"What? You quit ISB Hyderabad to become a writer?" I could not help but be impressed. *I wish I had the same dedication and motivation to prepare for Civil Services.*

"Yes, as a matter of fact, I did score 720 in GMAT and managed to get into ISB."

"You could have written the book after getting out of ISB. You would have had a good brand name and you could have used it as a marketing tool. Look at Chetan Bhagat. Do you think anybody would have read him if he wasn't from IIT and IIM?"

"You do have a point. But I have a different view of this. If you are a good writer and if your product is good, you will sell. Investing thirty lakhs in a degree after which I am going to do the same thing which I am doing now and for which you don't need the degree in the first place sounded like a waste of time and money for me."

She did have a point. I could not agree entirely with her, but I respected her decision and her dedication and commitment to writing.

"So, have you finished writing the book?"

"Yes the final draft is almost ready and now I will start looking for an editor."

"That is great. Your family must be very proud of you. It's not easy to write a novel."

"They have been moderately supportive. You know I am twenty-six and they want me to get married. There's just too much pressure. I think I'll be married by the end of this year."

A long silence followed as our eyes caught. That glance from her, I felt, had a message, a deadline of some kind. As if she was trying to tell me – 'If you want to make a move, remember you will have to marry me, and that too before December.'

I returned to my room, plopped on my bed and fell into a reverie. *Why wouldn't I love to marry a woman like Isha Bagga? She is everything I always wanted. Brilliant, beautiful, and we both love playing with words. I thought a novelist and a poet would make a good couple.*

I found myself smiling sheepishly when terror struck. I sat upright as my mind shoved in the reality and practicality of it all.

How I could possibly marry her? I did not have a job, I have to become an IAS and fulfil my dad's dream. God only knows how many more years I would need to clear this exam. Would it be another sad end to a potentially beautiful love story for me? I fell back on the bed, depressed.

Three days before my twenty-sixth birthday, the result for the staff selection commission (SSC) arrived. I had been allotted an Excise Inspector's job. Though it wasn't a job I was looking forward to, but still, it gave me a ray of hope. *Maybe I can get married after all.*

But first I would have to propose to Isha. What if she turns me down? Then what? If she loved me, she should accept me even if I was jobless. Excise Inspector was a group B job. Would she mind it?

Okay, hold on, let's calm down a bit. I cannot be planning a marriage when I don't even know whether she was in love with me or not!

▼

Gaurav tried to lay my doubts at rest. "Civil Serpentji, Excise Inspector is a very lucrative job. One of my friends is working as Excise Inspector in Gujarat. He must be earning more than most IIT and IIM graduates. Had you got an Income Tax Inspector's job, that would have been much better, of course."

"What do you mean?"

"There is more scope in Income Tax than in Excise." He smiled and continued, "Don't worry, she is a North Indian. She would prefer a government servant to a guy who is working in the private sector. If she or her parents know even a little about the money-making opportunities available in excise jobs, they would for sure not care if your job is group A, B or C," said Gaurav in his usual self-assured manner.

He was a man who could spot the silver lining even where I only saw dark clouds. I decided to break the news of getting a job and then confess my love to Isha.

▼

The next day after our class, I asked her out under the pretext of giving her a treat for landing a job.

"Close your eyes," I said after we sat down at Starbucks in Connaught Place.

"What is it?" she asked, a curious smile on her face.

"Close your eyes, Ish," I said with love in my eyes which she could easily see. As she closed her eyes, I took out a laminated piece of coloured paper on which I had written a poem for her and placed it in front of her. "Now you can open your eyes, Ish."

There were butterflies in my stomach, my heart had a manic pace of its own, and my hands shook as I waited to see her reaction. She picked up the laminated sheet and started reading…

Petite Novelina

To each pair of eyes that you comfort,
You mean something different.
As if a thousand lives you have lived,
You could be anything to anyone.
I wonder how you would like to be remembered.
To me, you are the sweet maiden
Who is busy writing my life on paper.
Or are you a story I am living
Through your dove-like eyes.
You leave me craving for more every time,
I tiptoe in the many worlds that you paint with words.
So write as much as you please,
For I shall read till it tires my soul,
And I will sleep on the lines of ink that you lay,
So I can wake up in your world, as I long to.
Very contagious you are when you smile,
That sweetness dripping from your eyes,
Your soft cheeks multiply your charm,
Have you been such a delight to watch all your life?
In fields of crops and green, I see,
Your flowery figure dancing in the wind,
Your sun- gilded hair in the morning,
You mesmerize and then evaporate.
So often, looking at you I feel,
Have I walked into a surreal dream?

"Thank you," was all she said. Her eyes and beautiful smile said more. I had managed to make a bit of room in her heart.

Two days later, we met on my birthday and she gave me the best gift I could have asked for. "I love you…" A symphony to my ears. "But for me, a relationship means commitment and nothing less than that," said Isha while sipping her coffee. "So I hope you are not wasting my time, because frankly, I don't have the time to waste on flings."

I looked deep into her eyes.

"My thoughts about relationships are the same as yours. I really do want to marry you, but is it possible to postpone the December deadline of your parents?"

"Why?"

"I will probably start working by December, not before that. Also, my Civil Service aspirations are still pending. If I don't clear this year, I would like to continue until I reach my goal. All I ask is that we marry next December. That way, I will at least have some savings or even better, I would have cleared UPSC."

"What you are saying is sensible. But our family astrologer studies my horoscope. He said the best time for me to marry is before this December. My parents are scared that I'll turn twenty-seven and won't find good marriage prospects. That's why the hurry."

"Ask them not to worry as I am ready to give you a commitment. We can take up an alternate arrangement also."

"What alternate arrangement?"

"We can get engaged by the end of December and marry next year."

"I don't think my parents will agree to that. I haven't heard people being engaged for more than a year. At max, we can stay engaged for six months and then we will have to marry."

"I see. But don't you realize we would still not be financially independent?"

"You won't have to worry about it. I'll take care of my expenses through writing and freelancing."

"After marriage, it's not going to be about you and me but about us, Isha."

Isha remained silent. I thought my last statement made her uncomfortable… as if I was trying to force the financial burden on her; a responsibility that is a man's domain.

"What do you mean by freelancing?" I asked, trying to lighten up the discussion.

"I used to work for a company before I decided to work full time on my novel. They love my work so much that they have asked me to join them whenever I feel like it. Since I can't work full time, they sometimes hire my services on a project basis, which doesn't involve too much time. I also work for some other clients on a part-time basis."

"So how is your novel progressing?"

"Well, actually, I wanted to tell you. I have zeroed in on a publishing house and hopefully, the novel should be out by the end of next month."

"Congratulations! That's wonderful news. Treat!"

"Sure! But there is a lot to be done. I have to shoot the trailer/teaser for the novel along with designing the website for the novel. Then I have to promote my book on social media by setting up a blog and twitter account. I think the real work will start after the book is released as I will have to take my book to the public and build an audience for my next book."

"Next book?"

"Yes. The book that I am going to get published is the first of a series of six books."

"What is the book about?"

"It's fiction, about the struggles of children in a competitive society. It's a story of inspiration, courage and hard work showing no matter where you are born, you can still make it big with hard work and achieve your dreams."

"Have you named your book yet?"

"Yes! I have named it *The Underdogs*."

"Nice name. I really wish to read it as soon as possible and get a signed copy."

"You will," she said and smiled.

After that meeting with Isha, things between us progressed at a rapid pace. Within a week we had our first kiss beneath the arch of Safdarjung Tomb and soon we were making out in my room in Old Rajinder Nagar. But soon, the very first signs of the weak foundation and the haste in our relationship began showing up.

We were in my bed, after our first lovemaking session, that I saw the beginning tears of separation in Isha's eyes.

"*Golu* Isha, you are so cute. You are my *motu* (plump) baby," I had said to her in a very playful manner.

Isha had turned her face away from me and buried it in the pillow. For a few minutes she remained in that position and then I tried to get her to turn to my side. I realized that she was in tears.

"What happened? Why are you crying?"

"Why are you calling me *motu*? Which girl likes to hear this after they make love for the first time? If you find me fat, why did you get into this relationship?"

"I just said it playfully. You are not fat at all. I was just trying to treat you like a little baby."

"You have been calling me *golu* a lot. It's irritating. When I was sitting at home working on my novel, I put on weight. I have been taunted about being jobless and gaining weight. I've been told so often that nobody would want to marry me, it haunts me. Stop calling me *motu* and *golu!* It's irritating and offensive."

"I called you *golu* because you have chubby cheeks. It had nothing to do with your weight, babes."

"I just want to tell you one thing. This is how my body is. The profession that I want to excel in is sedentary. I will put on weight since it requires a lot of sitting and if you have any issues with this, back out now. I won't blame you for anything."

It took some time for me to realize how sensitive and socially-conscious girls were towards their bodies and looks. Somehow I managed to convince her I wasn't concerned about her weight or her getting fat and that she should try to read me when I was just being playfully romantic with her. But it freaked me out a bit. I had to be extra careful now.

▼

The next week, we sat in my room eating chhole-kulche. The song Zombie by the Irish rock band, The Cranberries, was playing on my laptop.

"It's my favourite song," said Isha as she started humming the song.

"I love Dolores O'Riordan. Love her voice and her hairstyle."

"You love short hair?" asked Isha. She had suddenly stopped singing.

"Yes, I love girls with short hair. I think it will look good on you too, Isha."

"I used to have short hair in school."

"So why don't you give it a try again? I would love to see you in short hair."

"I will after marriage. For my marriage, I want long hair. I want to look like a typical Indian bride with long hair."

"That's up to you. I won't force you, but I think as a bride in short hair you would make quite a fashion statement." And I started showing her various short hairstyles on Google.

I was so excited about the prospect of seeing Isha with short hair that for the next couple of days I sent her many short hairstyle pictures. It had become a thing with me since I genuinely thought Isha was considering the change.

"Look at your extreme left, Isha. Do you see that redhead in short hair? That hairstyle will look extremely good on you."

"Okay, fine!" Isha said in a loud voice.

"Hey, what happened?"

"I am tired of listening to your short hairstyle talks. Can you give it a break?"

"Hey, I thought we were discussing the short hairstyle because you wanted to explore it too."

"Yes, I do plan to keep it after marriage, but the way you keep talking about it all the time makes me think you want me to cut my hair right now. If you wanted a girl with short hair, why didn't you find one to begin with?"

"Now where is this coming from? Please don't overreact."

"I am not overreacting! Why don't you understand me?"

"I do understand you."

"No you don't," she snapped.

I could see Isha's eyes filling up with tears again. My time with her that day didn't last that long. It was an uneasy goodbye.

That night we didn't call or message each other. Sometimes things don't add up in life even if you try to make it work. My relationship with Isha was turning out to be one such thing. I loved her, but somehow her behaviour was making me doubt my potential to make this love last.

I wanted the night all to myself without talking to Isha so that I could introspect on what exactly was going wrong. I just couldn't figure it out. It was a very unpleasant feeling to be giving your best to someone and things still not working out.

I somehow managed to sleep through this unpleasant feeling. The next day UPSC Mains results of 2012 were declared: I had flunked again. I went numb. I couldn't think of anything. I called my parents and told them that I had failed. The wave of sympathy that I received from them led me further into depression. My mother smothered me with her words of pity and my dad pretended as if nothing had gone wrong.

"It's just an exam. If not IAS, then you will do something better. Don't worry. I am there to support you," said my father, and followed it with, "but I still think you should give another attempt. I'll support you, don't worry about the money."

Obviously, what else was I going to do if not give another attempt? I was allotted Andhra Pradesh as Excise Inspector. I didn't know when exactly my joining letter would arrive since Andhra Pradesh was getting divided into two states, Andhra and Telangana. The joining date was uncertain. The more my family tried to sympathize with me, the more I felt like a loser. If this failure in Mains wasn't enough, Isha called me up right after I spoke to my parents.

"I wanted to talk to you about something. Are you free?"

"Yes," I blurted out in a feeble attempt to jolt out of my numbness.

"I think it's not working out. I tried thinking it through, but I think we rushed into this relationship," she said.

"What? What are you saying... not working... rushed... I don't even have the slightest idea... since when..." I struggled to make sense of things.

Before I could complete my sentence, she interrupted me. "I think I don't love you. Let's break-up before it hurts more," Isha said bluntly. I felt as if I was free-falling into a bottomless pit of darkness and depression.

"Okay," I said, and cut the call without waiting for Isha to say anything more.

I switched off my phone so that I could be left alone. But since the Mains results were declared, Balram paid me a visit and brought more sympathy with him, which led me into further self-pity. Gaurav turned up to offer his condolences over a smoke. I was six cigarettes down already by the time. He even offered me company for drinking, thinking it would help, but I just politely refused. I just wanted to be all by myself this time.

As I drowned in my misery, having lost all sense of time, I heard repeated knocks on my door. I looked at the table clock in front of me; it was way past midnight. *Who could it be?* It turned out to be Ankit.

"How was your result?" I asked him, although his face clearly told me that he had flunked too.

He didn't say anything. He just came and sat on my bed. "I would have ended my life today had it not been for Sakshi postponing her marriage for another UPSC attempt."

"Are you mad? You are going to end your life for an exam which essentially is a gamble?"

"It's not just about the exam. It's also about Sakshi."

"If her condition is for you to clear Civil Service for marriage, then better not marry such a woman."

"Why don't you understand? It's not her; it's her parents. They are not ready to wait. Also, the caste equation doesn't favour me."

"I really don't understand now. She isn't marrying you because you are not an IAS or because you belong to a lower caste?"

"Her parents are totally against marriage to any lower caste man. But she says if I get into IAS, then she might be able to reason it out with them." Ankit's voice had become louder as he said this. He was explaining this to me for the nth time. As always I found this reason confusing and absurd.

"Has she returned from London?"

"Yes, she has. Since her return, she has been sounding unsure about the prospect of our marriage. She has repeatedly been telling me the only chance that I have of marrying her is if I clear IAS. I just don't know what to do! I don't think I will be able to take the pressure for more than a year."

"You are taking unnecessary tension. Drink, my friend, and tomorrow you shall feel better."

"I get a feeling I have already lost Sakshi. There was a slight chance if I had cleared this year, but alas, once again I have failed. Just to make me feel better, she is saying she will try to postpone her marriage for another attempt, but I know it in my heart it's a lost cause." Ankit began sobbing.

I don't know how I managed to console him given that an hour ago, even I had felt like running away to someplace where nobody could find me.

31

The Astrologer

I was taken by surprise when my dad booked air tickets for me to come home for a week!

Within a few hours of reaching home, my dad drove me straight to an astrologer he had mentioned a few times. Mom accompanied us. All through the ride, he praised the accuracy of the astrologer's predictions about events and outcomes.

The confidence with which my parents discussed astrology belied the fact that in reality they had absolutely no knowledge of it and were solely banking on external popular sources.

It was irritating to be subjected to all this. What made it even more annoying was to be home just after a failure. The mountain of sympathy family members fling at you literally suffocates you. In the past, predictions of other astrologers my father had consulted, had turned out to be absolutely wrong.

His strategy was simple. He overlooked all the suggestions made by the astrologers that didn't favour his own wishes. He would overhype and magnify the slightest signs given by the astrologers that supported them.

I stared out of the car, pretending to listen. I was meeting an astrologer, a man who did not know a single thing about me and had never met me. That such a man got to decide what the course of my life would be, made me feel even more helpless than before.

We waited in the visitor's room. The astrologer charged five hundred rupees for five questions. A thin, tall, youthful man in his late thirties, emerged. He glanced at us and went into another room. After a few minutes, we were called inside.

"Namaskar! So, this is your boy," said the astrologer, whose name was Madhav. Then he started doing something on his computer. "Please check if his birth date and birth timing is correct. I went through the details you had submitted earlier." I saw the horoscope software on his computer screen generate my horoscope.

"You can start asking the questions," the astrologer said.

"Do you think he will clear UPSC Civil Service this year?"

He started looking at the horoscope on the screen. "It seems difficult. Even if he does clear, he will not be able to get a good rank. His 'Guru' is very weak. I told you this last time too." When I heard that, my temper rose. This man had predicted I wouldn't make it this time!

My mother asked, "Is there any puja or mantra to overcome his weak 'Guru' so that he can be successful in this exam?"

"Yes. Ask him to wear a *pukharaj* (yellow sapphire) in his right index finger. Also, his *kundli* shows that he is going to have a problem related to his throat. For that, he will have to wear another stone around his neck."

"Do you want to ask him any question?" my dad asked me.

"Is there any scope for me to go abroad?"

"Your horoscope says that the west direction is lucky for you. You will do well if you leave this country."

I looked at my dad waiting for a reaction. He shot back, "He wants to be a poet and a writer. Now you only tell me… millions of writers are just going around with a *jhola* with no source of income. What will he do if he becomes a writer?"

The astrologer gave me a mischievous smile, but said nothing.

My mother interrupted the silence. "Tell us something about his marriage."

"There is still time for his marriage. But the stars would be favourable for marriage only from January 2014 onward."

"Will they have a son or a daughter?" asked my mother in excitement.

"Most probably, it's going to be a boy."

I just wanted to get up and run. Here I was, jobless, and my parents were discussing my marriage and the sex of my future progeny! I suppose I should thank my stars they didn't ask him the exact date and time on which my future wife and I should have sex so that our son would be born under a suitable *nakshatra* to become an IAS officer!

"One final question, Madhavji. Should my son go for private-sector job or public sector job? Which would be beneficial for him?"

"Government sector jobs are the best."

"But you said it's going to be difficult for him to clear UPSC! Which government job are you talking about?"

"There are so many. Why doesn't he try for MPSC (Maharashtra public service commission)? UPSC is not the only way up. One of my friends started as a clerk in railways, but his computer skills allowed him to slowly rise up and now he is at a very high position in the railways."

Great! Now an astrologer is giving out career advice to a man who is an engineering and management graduate… and recommending he become a clerk! Since glaring at my parents would be an anti-climax, I just looked at them with a sweet smile. It gave me a lot of satisfaction to see that my smile thoroughly irritated my parents. *Gotcha!*

Without my father asking him any further question, the astrologer advised, "Since your son is an Engineer, he can also try for Indian Engineering Service (IES)."

Oh, how groovy! From clerk to an engineer! Moving up in the world! My sweet smile hitched back into place.

The car drive home wasn't easy. Dad had begun pestering me to prepare for IES, but I had no intention to. I had no interest in my Engineering subjects. I'd somehow managed to get a degree. Returning to it after all these years was not on, no matter what.

For all my stay at home and even till the point of my departure from the airport, both my parents were busy ramming the so-called career options down my throat. I really used the sweet smile a lot that visit.

▼

The moment I landed in Delhi, I heaved a sigh of relief. I was back to my heaven; my heaven of failure – Old Rajinder Nagar. I still wasn't used to the yellow sapphire ring on my right index finger. If I failed again, it would be proved that the path to success didn't go through a stone. I stared at the ring as the cab drove me into the narrow lanes of Old Rajinder Nagar. The stone shone and the lanes got darker.

On my way to the second floor, I bumped into Rajiv.

"Hey, how was your result? Did you clear Mains?" I asked.

"Yes, I cleared," he said unassumingly. A wave of unadulterated jealousy washed over me. *What the fuck! This louse cleared!! Dammit!*

It took me a few seconds to gather myself. *Wow. So newbies who have had just a few months of preparation can clear Mains in the first attempt. And guess who can't? Me!!!* I wanted the ground to swallow me.

"Congratulations and all the best for the interview," I said with a fake smile. But Rajiv didn't even look at me and just went down the stairs without saying thanks, or asking me about my result. *The arrogant SOB!*

Later that evening when I told Ankit about Rajiv's success in Mains, it filled him with self-doubt too. We questioned our potential. In a fresh surge of depression, Ankit declared suicide as the best option. I tried to divert him and talk about something else. I regretted telling him about Rajiv's success. I decided never to discuss anyone's success with Ankit.

32

Our Third Attempt

19 May, the date for the third Prelims was approaching, but my excitement was long dead. The Prelims had become a mere formality. I had stopped complaining about the paucity of time to prepare for this exam. It was going to be my third attempt. Before the Prelim exam, the result of last year's UPSC Civil Service exam was declared. Rajiv Ranjan Jha was AIR 41, IAS, in his first attempt at the young age of twenty-two. I went to congratulate him in his room. He had already vacated it the day before, as soon as he got the news of his selection! Of course, he left without bidding us goodbye! He remained a conceited, anti-social guy from start to finish. I hoped I would never have to deal with him again.

The day of 2013 Prelims arrived and here I was again at the exam centre, in the middle of a sea of unknown and nameless faces. Somehow they felt familiar: some smiling, some still peeping into books, as if last-minute studying would help. I heard someone calling my name. It was Rohini. The moment I saw her, I was reminded of Abhijeet.

"Good morning. How is the preparation for Prelims?"

"I don't know. I am just going through the motions. Sorry to hear that you could not clear the interview round last year, but I am sure this time around you would surely tame this exam."

"You know Abhijeet had cleared the Mains," Rohini said suddenly. "He scored well. Even if he had scored 100 marks in his interview, he would have been through."

I didn't know what to say. "Be strong, Rohini. I am sure you will fulfil Abhijeet's dream."

"I really don't care if I become an IAS officer or not. I want to know the higher purpose of life. Abhijeet had so many dreams. Without warning, he was gone. Didn't even take him one damn second! We all spend all our lives struggling to see those dreams materialize and fight for our beliefs. What is the purpose of these grand plans when there is no certainty of life? Who will teach us how to live every second and be grateful, how to love deeply and laugh like a child?" she asked. For some strange reason, I was deeply moved. But all I could do was to say a few hackneyed sympathetic words.

The 2013 Prelims was the easiest of all the prelims I had appeared for; I was surely getting to appear for Mains again.

It was almost July and my preparation for Mains was on track. Ankit called up one day, sobbing.

"Hey, what happened? Are you alright?" I asked him.

He continued to sob without saying anything. "Can we meet somewhere? I can't talk on the phone," he said when he calmed down a bit. We decided to meet at Safdarjung Tomb.

I arrived way too early to meet him, or maybe he was late, I wasn't sure. I sat inside the arches of Safdarjung tomb, my gaze wandering. All I could see was my past and beautiful memories of the time spent here.

This was the place I had met Sarah for the last time. That was where I had kissed Isha for the first time. Ankit had still not arrived. I tried calling him up, but he didn't take my call.

Just then, I saw Ankit at the far end of the entrance to the tomb.

"Sakshi broke up with me," Ankit said with swollen eyes.

Hadn't he seen that coming? "Oh…!" I managed to say. "Did you guys actually break-up or is she merely suggesting it?"

"We broke up," he said, his eyes filling up again.

"Ankit, I really think she was just suggesting it. Maybe she was overcome with guilt because of the kind of conditions that are being put on your relationship."

Ankit didn't say anything. I called Sakshi. Thankfully, she confirmed my theory.

Ankit multiplied his efforts to study with the possibility of heartbreak hanging over his head. He slept barely for four hours. His consumption of Red Bull grew. He started smoking too! I feared this would affect his health, but he didn't care. I lacked the moral right to say anything to him when I was doing it myself.

That year, except Sakshi, we had all cleared the Prelims. Ankit had begun drinking three to four cans of Red Bull every day! It was just a matter of time before the lack of sleep would start showing. Ankit was irritable most of the time and was way more abusive than I had ever seen him before.

He often told me about the fights he would have with Sakshi over silly things. Things got worse. He often threatened Sakshi with ending his life over the minutest of confrontations. Once Sakshi got so scared after Ankit stopped receiving her calls that she called me up to check on Ankit, fearing that he had done something to hurt himself.

It was sensitive of Sakshi to still be in the relationship despite Ankit's unreasonable behaviour. She was optimistic that Ankit's behaviour would change once he cleared the exam. She hoped Ankit would become an IAS officer and marry her.

We both prayed that this phase gets over soon and everything would end well. I had seen the ups and downs their relationship had endured, hence shared some of her optimism. When Sakshi failed to clear the Prelims, she drew emotional support from Ankit. It was her turn to be the sane and patient one now.

My own fear of failure and helplessness was a challenge to overcome. I focused on Ankit's miseries as if his pain was the escape, the cure for my pain.

▼

For the past three years, it seemed nothing had changed during my stay in Old Rajinder Nagar. June of 2010 felt like yesterday. The only thing that had changed along with my weight, the women I had loved and the syllabus of UPSC Civil Service was the hope I had, along with the gemstone I was wearing for luck.

In 2011, UPSC introduced CSAT for Prelims. Now in 2013, UPSC was again set to redefine the rules of the game called Mains, which would compel the lakhs of aspirants to completely change their exam preparation strategies, study materials needed, selection of optional paper and time management.

UPSC had decided a year ago to do away with one of the two optional subjects. I had decided to stick with Psychology, as my scores in Philosophy remained poor.

Ankit's story was funnier. He paid forty thousand rupees for the Public Administration coaching for the second time and ended up getting 40 marks in Paper-I, his lowest score in Public Administration so far!

Along with the removal of one optional subject from the Mains syllabus, the other change that was made was the introduction of a new subject paper called Ethics and Integrity.

It was going to be interesting to see as to what exactly and on what parameters they would set the question paper. If measuring the ethical integrity of the candidate was the real purpose of UPSC, by introducing this new paper I wasn't sure how successful they were going to be.

However, in Old Rajinder Nagar you could hear people talking about ethical corruption which was based on the principle of *Joh dey uska bhi bhala jo na dey uska bhi bhala* (bless those who bribe and also bless those who don't).

As a result of all the above changes, the role of optional paper got reduced, and the balance shifted towards General Studies. Many aspirants celebrated as they thought that the changes would provide a level playing field for all. But the big question remained, who would these changes favour? Would it favour the Veterans or the Freshers? Will the generalists gain or the specialists prevail?

It was winter already. I prayed for it to be my last winter here. After Guwahati not helping my case, this year I decided to write Mains from Delhi.

Because of the changes made in the syllabus, the dates had been pushed back. Exams were going to start from 1 December this year.

I didn't have the time or the money to go for Ethics coaching class. I bought Crack IAS Ethics notes from the market for three thousand rupees. However, by the end of November, the notes mostly lay unused. The Mains were going to start from 1 December, and I wasn't mentally ready for it, as usual.

Somehow with the help of Red Bull, cigarettes and sleeping pills, I managed to pull through this one too. Knowing the answer or not was immaterial; something or the other had to be written and the pages filled. All I remember was that the weightage for papers changed and each paper was for 250 marks instead of the usual 300 marks. That didn't reduce the amount of writing needed. On the contrary, it seemed to have increased.

As usual, after the Mains, I wondered if I could have done something different… something which would ensure success. While my mind had accepted defeat, knowing the result would not be any different, my heart was hoping for a miracle.

33

The Kurd

For a week after the Mains, I was bedridden. A terrible throat infection compounded with the side-effects from the antibiotics I took for my throat had made me weak as a kitten.

The sudden stop to my Red Bull and cigarette consumption made me feel lifeless. Quitting sleeping pills kept me awake. I wanted to sleep, but my restless mind wouldn't let me. My lips were swollen and my body felt as if I had been wrung out to dry. I had ulcers in my dry-as-sand-paper mouth and my ears burned. I was sick and the mirror was witness to my sorry state.

The new Samsung tab I had bought to replace my ageing Windows phone, was my only companion. I watched movies, listened to songs, read eBooks and yes, got addicted to Facebook. I killed time by keeping a check on what my batch-mates from Engineering and MBA were doing in their lives.

I spent hours prowling around their profiles, scrutinizing their status updates and pictures on Facebook. I regretted my decision of going for UPSC Civil Service preparation instead of a private-sector job. I made a lot of new Facebook friends; the more friends I made, the emptier I felt. Desperate to alleviate my feelings of loneliness, I sent and received friend requests to and from random strangers.

One such friend request I got was from a Turkish girl of Kurdish ethnicity. Her name was Hazal Demir. Her English was poor. Apparently, she had read one of my comments on a Turkish page dedicated to the German philosopher Friedrich Nietzsche and so decided to send me a friend request.

She belonged to a different culture and spoke a different language. I was happy for the free lessons about her way of life while remaining stuck in my hole in Old Rajinder Nagar. I wondered if it was the same for her too.

She was delighted to learn of my interest in poetry and asked me to write a poem for her. I told her that I would be happy to, but for that, I would love to know more about her family, her childhood, her friends, her nature and her likes. She happily obliged.

Hazal was excited and curious about India. We talked about everything. Once while discussing languages, I told her how Hindi and Turkish had a thousand similar words, since kings of Turkish origin ruled over India for close to three hundred years. She offered to teach me Turkish; I offered to teach her English.

She was the youngest of six sisters and five brothers. She was twenty-four and in the first year of her Engineering course. She wasn't good in studies, she confessed.

Even after I went to bed with a final goodnight, she kept messaging. I would mute the message notifications but my mind would not let me sleep. I kept checking if Hazal was still awake.

My obsession with Hazal was growing. I confessed this to Gaurav, which made him laugh. I never had a foreign friend before and all this excitement I was going through seemed justified.

Every morning I would wake up with excitement to read her messages. She sent me Neruda's poems, her favourite songs and interesting pictures of her villages and her sister's children.

One morning while I was still catching up on the messages I had received after I fell asleep, she asked me whether I would like to have a video chat with her. I could feel my heartbeat racing. My reply was in the affirmative.

I spent the whole day checking the Facebook messenger to see if she had replied. I would time and again read and re-read our old chat. Finally, my eyes were tired so I decided to take a quick nap in the evening.

It was the end of December and Delhi was freezing. As I started to doze off, I heard the message notification on Facebook. It was Hazal!

"*Merhaba. Nasilsin?*" Hazal asked in Turkish.

"*Bende iyiyim. Sen nasilsin?*" I replied in whatever little Turkish she taught me.

"*Iyiyim.* What you doing?"

"Waiting for your message," I replied candidly.

"We chat you tonight on Skype. *Tamam?*" she said in broken English mixed with Turkish that I would understand.

"*Tamam.*"

"*Simdi* I will rest. *Gorusuruz.* Will meet on Skype at 22.00 India time and 7.30 Turkiye time," she said.

"*Tamam* Hazal. *kendine iyi bak. Gorusuruz* on Skype." I replied in broken Turkish.

"*Seni ozledim. Gorusuruz.*" I didn't know what *seni ozledim* meant. Hazal had never taught me, so I Google translated it. It meant "I miss you". I was literally filled with joy!

"*Ben de seni ozledim,*" I replied back after translating "I miss you too" in Turkish. But by that time she had logged out of Facebook.

I was very excited. I wanted to look good so I rushed to a high-end salon to get a stylish haircut and a shave. My unorganized long beard had to be got rid of; it was an important guise for my *too-busy-studying* charade I put up for my family. *Why not get a face massage too?* I had never pampered myself so much before. My wallet didn't share my excitement for my video chat as I doled out a thousand bucks.

After my return, I still had an hour left so I decided to take quick steam from the steamer I had bought for my sinus problem. I loved inhaling the steam as it made me feel fresh. I would often take steam even if I didn't have a blocked up sinus.

With only half an hour to go, I took a quick bath and was ready, waiting for Hazal to contact me. Then I suddenly realized that I didn't have a Hotmail account or Skype account! I hurriedly created the accounts. Hazal didn't show up.

My anxiety was at its peak. *Would she find me good looking or would she stop talking to me after seeing me?* I spent quite a lot of time making faces in the mirror to assure myself that I looked passably good no matter what the expression. I did everything possible to create a good first impression.

It was 22:15 and she was late. *Perhaps she fell asleep or is stuck with some work. Meanwhile, let me check if Ankit Gupta and Sakshi Singh are on Facebook too. I have known them for three years now and yet I don't know how I forgot to add them to my Facebook friend list.*

I searched for Ankit and there he was. I instantly sent him a friend request. As I was going through his profile, I saw that his last activity was in January of 2010! There were barely any pictures. It was the same with Sakshi. I sent her a friend request as well. She had many 'missing you badly' and 'happy birthday' messages on her Facebook wall but her last activity was way back in 2007! *How have these people managed to stay offline from Facebook for such a long time? They are truly dedicated to UPSC!*

Before I could mull over this anymore, I saw Hazal's message on Facebook messenger asking me for my Skype ID. Soon we were video chatting on Skype. Hazal was gorgeous. Her golden hair, warm brown eyes and a perfectly chiselled supermodel face, made me feel inferior.

The very first time we video-chatted, we didn't voice chat but kept texting each other with the video on. Hazal was trying to teach me basic Turkish. This video chat went on for hours and even when Gaurav knocked on my door for a cigarette break, I didn't open the door. He knew about my video chat plans so, after a few knocks, he left.

After a while, my Internet connection began to falter and we had to stop our video chat. *Bloody hell! What else could you expect from a developing country like India where people don't even have proper access to toilet and drinking water?*

Hazal and I chatted for another hour on Facebook messenger and she continued teaching me basic Turkish. That night after we finished our chatting, I was so mesmerized with Hazal that I began writing a new set of poems that I had promised her.

The last poem that I had written was for Isha, before Prelims. It had been more than five months and now again, here I was, inspired by another woman!

Questions to A Maiden

Do you believe in holy books?
In the priests with serious looks?
In the god in thy neighbourhood?
They all predicted that you would come.
Do you believe in nursery rhymes?
In the gospels of ancient times?
In the sweet language of silence?
In the religion of love?
Do you believe in prayers and promises?
In the power of shooting stars?
In the hour of miracles and wishes?
In all the blessings in goodbye kisses?
Do you believe in heaven and hell?
In the kingdom of gods and angels?
Somewhere they say you belong,
Do you?
Do you believe in holy spirits?
That keeps you safe and warm,

From all the worldly harm.
Do you believe in committing sins?
Do you believe in tricks and magic?
In stories that end up tragic?
In signs and science?
In divine saints and sweet scents?
In colours of strawberries, rainbows,
Butterflies and chocolates?
Or are your fingers still crossed in your pockets?
Do you believe in love?

Hazal was very excited when I told her that I had written some poems for her. She wanted me to send the poems instantly on Messenger but I had other plans. Poems always looked good on paper, not a computer screen. I wanted to make them a little more personalized. I was apprehensive whether she would give me her address so I could send my handwritten poems to her. After all, we were random strangers on the internet. Fortunately, she gladly shared her address, though I had no idea what the address meant except for the pin code.

▼

I bought glitter and sketch pen, coloured A4 size card paper and got to work. Four poems handwritten in sketch pens of different colours on coloured card paper and then I decorated each one of them with designs of rainbows and butterflies in glitter. I patiently waited for the glitter to dry and then I got the sheets laminated.

Hazel's birthday was on 7th February. It was already mid-January. I got her a birthday card and a small picture book of historical monuments of India. This was all that could fit in an envelope of a size slightly bigger than an A4 size paper. The DHL, Blue Dart and other private courier services were charging three thousand rupees for the parcel to be delivered to Turkey. This was very expensive for me so

I decided to send the package through Speed Post. It cost me only seven hundred rupees, two hours of standing in a long queue, and my patience to follow all the procedures required.

After reaching home, I sent Hazal the picture of the parcel on Facebook, along with the tracking number of the parcel. Later that evening when she saw the message she was delighted.

"How many days parcel come?" asked Hazal in her broken English.

"Within seven days," I said, as was told to me by the old man at the counter.

"*Tessekur ederim Arkadasim*. I wait."

Tired by the afternoon activity, after chatting for some more time that night, I retired to bed. I went to bed a happy man dreaming about how Hazal would fall madly in love with me after reading the poems. But I wondered if she would understand them. She hardly knew any English. *It doesn't matter. Love is beyond language and when she would see the poems she would understand.*

The next morning when I woke up, my eagerness to read Hazal's messages was met with a rude shock. She had deactivated her Facebook account and this was her final message.

"*Kanim arkadasim.* Don't forget me ever. I will miss you. *Hoscakal*."

34

The Prostitute

Hazal's sudden disappearance left me feeling bereft and baffled. Now that she had her poems, she decided to leave? I felt used.

In desperation, I bought an international calling pack for my cell phone. I tried calling her on the cell number she had given me, but it was switched off. All through the day, I went through our Facebook chats a hundred times. What I thought to be a love story was now a classic case of being fooled on the internet. *Whoever she was… she must be tickled pink with the smooth execution of her trick. It must have entertained her thoroughly to not only have me write poems about her to flaunt but to think I actually took the trouble to mail the handwritten copies all the way to Turkey!*

Over and over, I asked myself why she would do it. I sent her a mail expressing my anger over the way she treated me. It was over a week and I had received no reply from her. Gaurav asked me every day about Hazal and whether she had received the poems. As if things with Hazal weren't depressing enough, my parents had begun calling me every day, asking about the Mains result.

I didn't know whom to confess to about the fool I had made of myself over the internet. From being a saviour angel who took away my mind from the pain of UPSC, Hazal had turned into a witch for me. I cursed her and hid my pain in the rum I consumed. Now I was in greater pain than ever. The fear of yet another failure at UPSC Mains result made it worse.

First Sarah, then Isha and now Hazal. I had heard about men playing with the feelings of women, but for me, it was the opposite. Whenever I was about to dive into a pool of self-pity, the memory of the girl who I had broken up with, without even a goodbye, came back to haunt me.

Was it karma then? If it was karma, I should have been punished only once, and it should have been over when Sarah left me. This isn't fair! I have never committed any grave crime towards any woman.

I needed a shoulder to cry on. Who else, but Ankit?

▼

"I am such a committed guy, very loyal and caring. I don't even look at other girls. I don't even want to sleep with Sakshi before marriage. But she just doesn't care about any of it," said Ankit after he was already quite a few drinks down.

He continued, "That Turkish bitch of yours is no different. The world over, girls as the same. Good men like us get fooled all the time and evil men even after sleeping with ten different girls still manage to get the most loyal and prettiest girls." He suddenly looked at me, drunk on alcohol and anger he said, "Let's be evil."

I was sloshed. I'd had twice the amount of alcohol Ankit had. Already messed up in my head, what Ankit said made perfect sense to me. I nodded sagely at him.

"I wasted my youth studying for one or the other exam. No fun, no dating. I didn't even drink or smoke. I never touched a single girl, leave alone betraying anyone. Look what life has done to me. But today I want to live. I just want to break free today. Let's go!"

Without asking him where, I followed him quietly. Memories of Hazal were eating me up. I didn't care where we were going. We were going to break free, that's all!

On the way, Ankit cursed Sakshi, the UPSC exam and almost everything else. I listened to him, paralyzed with drink and depression. My drunkenness only accentuated what he said.

We reached some place of which I had only a vague memory. Drinking on an empty stomach had made me dizzy. I remember seeing a theatre on the way. I hung on to Ankit's arm. I was feeling weak and felt as if I was swinging instead of walking. But Ankit was walking firmly, even though he too had drunk far more than his usual capacity. I vaguely remember reading the name of the road; it was named after some swami.

Ankit guided me through into a lane where shady looking men were standing around. Ankit spoke to one of them who took us to a building which must have had three floors. We made our way to some room on the second floor of that building with the man leading the way.

Women were standing on the passage and on every floor, shabbily dressed but with heavy makeup. They looked at us and smiled. Some of them were even calling us and making strange gestures, which I couldn't interpret. I was still thinking about Hazal.

Finally, we were there, right in front of a room and Ankit asked me to go inside the room. He was still talking to the guy who escorted us there. Before entering the room, I asked him, "Why are we here?"

"To celebrate Hazal's birthday and the birthdays of all those women who made our life hell. Now get inside and enjoy," he said with a sad, drunken smile and went back to his negotiations.

When I entered the room alone, I saw a young girl dressed in salwar kameez with very heavy makeup. It was around six in the evening and it had begun to get dark. The room was lit with a dim yellow bulb. The girl stood up and walked up to me and helped me to the bed.

"Babuji, can I get something for you to drink?" was the last thing I remember the girl asking me. I just nodded my yes. My head was feeling very heavy. I was losing my senses and I had no more strength.

I fell flat on the bed and passed out before the girl could bring me a drink.

When I regained consciousness, the girl was sitting on the only chair right in front of me, reading something. I was still in the zone of senselessness. I sat up groggy and confused. My wallet was missing!

I sprang from the bed and saw my wallet along with my mobile phone on the makeup table along with a cup of chai and something wrapped in newspaper.

"Alokji, would you like to have chai and eat something? It will make you feel better," said the girl, who must have been in her early 20s.

How did she know my name? And why were my wallet and mobile phone not in my pocket but on the table? Ankit was nowhere to be seen. I wanted to call Ankit but the phone battery was dead.

My head was still spinning. *Who is this girl and why am I here in the first place?* I remembered drinking with Ankit in my room, and then him taking me to someplace. I saw this girl before passing out.

Seeing the look on my face, the girl said, "Alokji, you need not be worried. Have this tea and samosa, you will feel better."

"Have you seen my friend, Ankit, who brought me here?" I asked her.

"No, I haven't. I thought you came here alone after getting drunk."

"Why are my wallet and mobile phone not in my pocket?"

"Because I wanted to steal your money and mobile," she said firmly and this was enough to get me back to my senses. I immediately checked my wallet and nothing was missing in it.

"All the money is in here. Why haven't you stolen anything then?" I asked her.

"I even wanted to steal the gold ring that you are wearing with that gemstone in it, but it wouldn't come off your finger," she said, mocking me. I didn't find it funny. My head was still pounding.

"When I was about to take the money from your wallet, I saw your driving license and your name on it. Your name sounded very familiar, someone I had heard of from a loved one. First I thought that you might be someone different, but then I saw your address on the driving license. It mentions that you are from Nagpur. So I decided not to steal the money but instead ask for help directly. I hope you will help me escape this place. You will, won't you, Alokji?"

The way she took my name felt as if she had known me for years. "Where is this place? And who are you?" I think I knew both the answers.

"Alokji, you are at a brothel in GB road and I am a prostitute."

"How do you know me?" I asked, still not coming to terms with the situation I was in.

"My brother knew you. Once he had mentioned you on the phone to us."

"I have no friend whose sister is a prostitute," I shouted back at her. I thought she was trying to get me into some kind of trouble. I was scared. The police are known to frequent such places and make arrests.

"I wasn't born into this trade. Back in the village, my family was poor but respectable. As a matter of fact, people like you make us prostitutes. No woman is born a prostitute but made into one by men and sometimes by other women." She said this in a low, cold, dejected voice and tears started rolling down her cheeks. Seeing her cry, I offered her my handkerchief. I felt guilty of the charges she pressed against men like me. I was angry at myself for being in this situation in the first place and cursed Ankit for getting me here. It was his plan.

"I am sorry. I didn't mean to say you were always a prostitute."

"Destiny is a funny thing. Instead of meeting you at your room in Old Rajinder Nagar, we are meeting here in this brothel. Who would have thought, Alokji?"

"What was the name of your brother?"

When she told me, I was flabbergasted.

35

Her Story

"I am Rashmi, Manish Pandey's sister, the guy who used to be your neighbour in Old Rajinder Nagar. Do you remember Manish bhaiya?" she whispered.

I had heard from Gaurav about Manish's missing sister. Finding her in a brothel of all places left me dumbstruck. All I could do was nod.

"I am not a thief, Alokji. I wanted the money to run away from here and go back to my parents. They are old and alone."

It broke my heart to hear her say that. My eyes filled up and a lump clogged my throat. I hadn't the heart to tell her of the misfortune that had fallen on her parents.

I swallowed hard. "Why did you run away from your parents?" I asked, my voice torn to shreds. *Was there no end to this family's tragedies? Why god, why?!*

"I had to find a job. There was a huge debt on my family. We had borrowed money for my elder sister's marriage and for Manish bhaiya's studies, but they killed my elder sister and bhaiya passed away suddenly. The money lenders were harassing my family. After bhaiya, both my parents gave up. I couldn't bear to watch them wither away right before my eyes. That's why I decided to find work in Delhi so we could pay off the debt."

"How did you end up in this profession?" I couldn't help asking.

"I was tricked into it by a man from my village. Jamal promised me a data-entry job in some small computer firm in Gurgaon. When I reached New Delhi railway station, a man called Raju came to pick me up. He first took me to an unknown location somewhere in Noida. I stayed for a week with four other women who had also come for a data-entry jobs. He visited us every day to keep a check on us and to see if we needed anything. Everything, including food, was provided for.

"One day we asked Raju when the job would start. He told us that some documentation work was pending and that the job would begin from next week. On the pretext of documentation, he took all our identity cards, including the various educational and birth certificates I was carrying.

"I was thrilled and so were my parents when I called to tell them I had found a job. That was the last time I ever spoke to them. I don't know in what condition they must be." Then she started crying, covering her mouth so that no one could hear her sobbing. Until that moment, I couldn't have imagined that a pair of human eyes could hold such deep misery in them.

Overwhelmed by her sorrow, which seemed intensely personal to me, I hugged her, tucking her head under my chin protectively.

She said, "The next morning, after I last spoke to my parents, I woke up to find myself in this very room, lying barely conscious and bleeding. I knew I had been drugged, raped and brought here. Raju must have mixed some drug in our dinner. The other girls were also missing. I never saw them again."

"You don't have to tell me all this. It would be painful for you, Rashmi."

"You have to listen. Someone will have to listen. I cannot keep my pain buried any longer. I beg you to listen, Alokji."

I held her hands tightly, squeezing them to show my support.

"They had taken away my mobile phone and I wasn't allowed to contact anyone. Many men visited me every day. If I protested, I was beaten up and told I would be killed if I didn't do what I was told or if I tried to escape. They even filmed me having sex with men while I was drugged. Time and again they threatened to send my sex video to my family or release it on the internet. After a few weeks of beating and getting raped, I gave in to this life of prostitution.

"I have no money. They take away whatever little customers give me. I no longer have any identity card or education certificate. It's been more than a year now. I have been trying to escape from here with the help of a customer, but once they've had their fun, they don't care to get involved.

"Today when you entered drunk and passed out on the bed, I thought this would be my chance, so I took out your wallet and mobile to make my escape, contact my parents and tell them where I am. I am not a thief, Alokji. You have to believe me. Will you please tell my parents I am stuck here? Will you please help me?" Sobbing, she fell to my feet.

I wiped her face with the already wet handkerchief.

"Hold yourself together, Rashmi. You have been incredibly brave all this while. I promise you that I will save you from this wretched place, no matter what. Just act normal in front of the pimp and pretend that I was just another customer. Rest I'll handle."

I hugged her and took leave of her. I couldn't bear to tell her about her parents' sad demise. She had enough on her plate for now.

I signalled her all the best with my thumb and left the room. When I descended the stairs, I met the person with whom Ankit had been speaking earlier.

"You took a lot of time, Sirjee. I think you enjoyed a lot. I gave you the best piece we have. She provides best services to everyone. You were lucky that she wasn't making someone else happy," said the man, after spitting out the gutka he was chewing.

"I enjoyed a lot. I want no one else from now on." I took out four thousand rupees I had withdrawn just the day before and gave it to him. What I paid him was thrice of what he expected. "Keep this, I will give you more when I come tomorrow. Make sure she is not tired when I come."

The extra money made the man jubilant. Puffing at his bidi, he said, "Consider this girl as yours from now, Sirjee. Whenever you come, just ask for me and I'll arrange for her to be at your service."

"What is your name and what is her name?"

"Sirjee, my name is Bhagwan and her name is Baby Doll. Please note down my number. If you find someone else here when you come, just give him my reference and say you want Baby Doll." It didn't sound like his real name, but I didn't care. I left.

I wanted to call up Ankit to ask where he was. I was really angry with him for having disappeared though I no longer wanted to shout at him. If he hadn't brought me here, I'd never have found Rashmi.

As it is my phone was dead, so I couldn't contact Ankit or Gaurav immediately. I made my way back to my room, my mind and emotions in deep turmoil. I couldn't save Manish, but I had to save his sister. And I knew exactly what I needed to do.

36

The Rescue

As soon as I reached my room, the first thing I did was to put my phone on charging and then I rushed to Gaurav's room. I could hear him talking on his phone as I approached his door. I started banging on his door like a madman.

"What is the matter? I am speaking to my mother," he shouted from inside.

"*Behenchod,* open the fucking door...!" I kicked the door while I banged on it.

He opened the door slightly and said, "You dickhead! I am discussing something very important with my mother," and slammed the door on my face.

"I found Manish's sister!" I shouted at the top of my voice. As soon as Gaurav heard this, he opened the door and switched the phone off immediately, after telling his mother he would call her back, for something urgent had surfaced.

"What are you saying? Where and when?" He stared at me in disbelief. "Tell me, tell me dammit! Don't just stand there!" he said in an agony of desperation. I wasn't surprised. I'd have been too.

"In a brothel. She was forced into prostitution and we have to save her by hook or by crook," I said.

"What the fuck!!" his face had drained of colour.

The noise woke Balram too. He came to ask us to be quiet. I grabbed his arm and made him sit. He knew about Manish but not about the misfortune that had fallen on his family. I narrated the whole sad story to him, telling of the misfortunes that had fallen on Manish's family after his death.

"How did she land in that brothel?" asked Gaurav impatiently as soon as I finished telling Balram about Manish's family.

I told Gaurav and Balram everything Rashmi had told me. Gaurav's eyes brimmed over. He shared a close relationship with Manish. I knew he had still not got over Manish's death.

"What were you doing in the brothel?" Balram asked me in the midst of all the drama.

I then told them both the events that had led to the visit.

"Ankit took me with him to GB Road. I didn't even know such a place existed in Delhi."

"You mean you...no...whaaaaaaatt!" said Gaurav.

Figuring out what he was thinking, I said, "No! It isn't as you are thinking! I was completely drunk even before we left my room. As soon as I entered Rashmi's room, I crashed on her bed and passed out. It was only when I came to my senses did I come to know that the prostitute Ankit had brought me to was Manish's sister!"

The room fell silent, all of us grappling with our own thoughts. No one had any more questions to ask.

"Guys, we must help her out of that brothel and rehabilitate her," I said.

"Yes, we must!" both of them said in unison.

"What do you plan to do next?" Balram asked.

"First thing tomorrow morning, we will go to the police and file a complaint," I said.

"It's not that easy. Why do you think brothels are still working? It's because of the blessings of the police. Otherwise, these places would have been shut down long ago. Police gets protection money from such places. If you go and complain to them, chances are that they won't register your complaint," Gaurav said.

"Can we approach any NGO who rescues women forced into the sex trade?" I asked.

"Yes, this is a better idea. But does anyone know of such an NGO? Hope we knew some influential person who could help us out." The moment Gaurav said this, we stared at Balram. After all, his father was the leader of opposition in Chhattisgarh assembly. Congress had been ruling in Delhi for the past fifteen years.

"Yes, friends, I'll talk to my father first thing in the morning. But what if he asks uneasy questions like how do I know Rashmi and why am I concerned with this particular case out of nowhere?"

We were again in a fix. I had met Balram's father once. He was a generous and a polite man, but very religious, like Balram. I doubted whether he would help if he concluded that Balram was into prostitution and it would be even worse if he pinned Balram's failure in the first exam attempt to this.

Balram jumped to his feet and said, "Don't worry, I'll figure out a way. Leave it to me."

We tried forcing him to tell us what he had in mind but he wouldn't budge. Gaurav and I gave up.

"Let's sleep, friends. It's already 2 a.m. Tomorrow is a critical day for us," said Balram.

I came back to my room. I immediately called Ankit. I was still wondering what made him leave me like this at the brothel. How could he leave me at such a place? Much to my surprise, he received my call.

Before I could say anything, Ankit said, "I am very sorry, Alok. I left you there at the brothel. I tried calling you later on, but your phone was switched off."

"Why did you leave me there and disappear suddenly? What happened?"

"After I arranged for a girl for you and saw you going in, I got into another room. But Sakshi's face flashed in front of my eyes, her voice filled up my head. I felt horribly guilty. I couldn't imagine being with any other girl. I ran away. I am very sorry I took you to the brothel and made you dip your feet in evil."

"I didn't have sex with that girl you sent me to."

"So why was your phone switched off?"

"That's because the battery died. I passed out as soon as I entered the room. You know how high I was on an empty stomach."

"Yes, brother. I am sorry once again for what happened. It's very late. I will sleep now that I know you have reached home safe. Goodnight."

"Goodnight." I was tired but my mind was all messed up and my eyes were waiting for the first light of dawn. Before going to bed, I checked Facebook to see if Hazal had returned. She hadn't. Dejected, I went to bed but kept awake until morning.

Rashmi's unfortunate story didn't let me sleep. I got out of bed when Balram knocked at 9 a.m. I opened the door to see him enter Gaurav's room and I followed him.

"My dad has agreed to help us," he announced.

"How did you manage it?" I asked surprised and delighted.

"I'll tell you later. Get ready quickly. My dad has given the name of some NGO called the 'Rescue Foundation'; they will be contacting us. It will coordinate with the Delhi Police and help us get Rashmi out of the brothel."

"But what about the police? Will they cooperate with us?" Gaurav asked.

"Yes, dad has taken care of that too. He spoke to the Police Commissioner of Delhi personally. The Commissioner has directed some police team under the supervision of an ACP to help us. Now, let's not waste any time. Alok, will you be able to identify the building and the room in which Rashmi has been kept?"

"I'm sure I will be able to."

"Okay, friends, so we leave in another hour. Get ready. Let's do it so that Manish's soul rests in peace," said Balram.

Balram had never met Manish or any of his family members, but the manner in which he had gone out of the way to help us was really praise worthy. It must have been difficult for him to persuade his father to help us.

"God bless you and your father for helping us," I said to Balram as we made our way in the Metro to the Rescue foundation NGO office near Connaught Place.

Balram looked at me and said, "You were there for me when I needed your help last time around, Alok. This is the least I could do. I hope we succeed this time at least."

We met with the investigation officer of Rescue Foundation, Mr Patel. "Look, this is a very noble job you guys are doing of rescuing a soul in distress. But we have to follow the proper procedure to prove that she was forced into prostitution and has not entered the profession on her own. I hope she does not change her stand later."

"She is our friend's sister and we know she comes from a respectable family," Gaurav said with intensity.

"Then how did she land up in the brothel?" asked Mr Patel.

I had to narrate the whole story again. Gaurav couldn't bear to hear it again so he went out of the office. He entered with a woman in uniform just as I was finishing. She introduced herself as ACP Chhaya Sharma.

"It looks like a promising case, madam," said Mr Patel, standing up to greet Ms Sharma. We all stood up and shook hands with her.

"So what's the background of the case?" asked Ms Sharma. She looked like a very young IPS officer, maybe of our age.

I narrated the whole story again. When she knew I was preparing for Civil Services, she made a cogent remark. "What kind of Civil

Servant will you become if you end up in a brothel after getting drunk? We need Civil Servants who are in control."

I felt ashamed of myself. I wanted to justify myself by telling her that it was because of my friend that I landed up there, but I didn't want to start a blame game lest it made me look stupid.

"Let's get over with this case, Mr Patel," said Ms Sharma.

Mr Patel said, "So, boys, here is how it's going to be. We have investigators who visit the brothels, or any other place where forced prostitution is being carried out, as decoy customers. Thereafter they conduct in-brothel counselling whereby they obtain the consent of the victim to be rescued from the torture and forced prostitution. The rescue team then conducts a raid on the premises and rescues the victim."

"How many days will it take?" Gaurav asked.

"Anywhere between two days to a month," said Mr Patel.

"It won't take more than two days," said Ms Sharma, interrupting Mr Patel. "The Chief Commissioner of Police, Delhi, himself called me and asked me to wind up the case as soon as possible. It seems like one of you guys is well-connected."

We didn't say anything.

"You come with us and help us to identify the pimp and the place where this girl is held captive," said Ms Sharma, pointing towards me.

▼

Two police jeeps were waiting for us. Ms Sharma, Mr Patel and the three of us got into one Jeep and the second police jeep followed us. When we reached GB road, I recalled the Swami Marg signboard which I had seen. I asked Ms Sharma to halt the Jeep, but she didn't. She took the vehicle a good long distance from the place before parking it. She said she didn't stop there so as to avoid suspicion on the part of the pimps that it was a raid or inspection. A policeman dressed in plain clothes got down from the other jeep. It wasn't difficult to guess that he was the decoy customer who was going to visit the brothel.

"He is Sub-Inspector Ritesh Yadav. We have trained him well in carrying out such inspections, and he has previous experience in such rescue acts," said Mr Patel as he introduced me to the policeman. "Now lead him to the brothel premises and give him the necessary information he asks for."

As Mr Yadav and I made our way towards the brothel, I told him to look for the pimp called Bhagwan, and ask him for the girl called Baby Doll. In case Bhagwan was not there, he should just give Bhagwan's reference and ask for the girl.

From a distance, I could see the building and as we approached nearby, I saw that Bhagwan was missing, and some lady who looked like a eunuch was sitting on a chair at the entrance of the building.

"Bhagwan isn't there sitting today. Will it be difficult now?" I asked the policeman.

"It will be easier. If Bhagwan was there and I had asked specifically for Baby Doll, he would have smelled something fishy and given me some other girl for service. Now it would be relatively easier. Don't worry; I'll handle it from here."

"Thank you, sir. She is on the second floor. All the very best."

Mr Yadav smiled and asked me not to worry. I saw him walking towards the building. At the entrance of the building, he got into a conversation with the eunuch sitting there. There was some animated conversation going on from both sides, and it wasn't getting over. This made me nervous.

But then the eunuch accompanied Mr Yadav and I could see her take Mr Yadav to the second floor.

My phone rang; Gaurav was calling me. "Come back to the police jeep immediately. We are waiting for you." The voice of Ms Sharma calling from Gaurav's mobile took me by surprise.

I wanted to stay back until Mr Yadav emerged out of the building, but I had instructions to return, so I did. On the way back, I saw Bhagwan coming from the other side. I tried to avoid him, but he recognized me. My heart began thumping. I hoped that the rescue operation wouldn't go wrong now because of this chance meeting.

"Sirjee, remember me? You had come last night too. Did you visit Baby Doll again?" Bhagwan's alcoholic breath hit my nose.

I just nodded, trying to avoid using words.

"I knew you would visit us again soon. Such a piece Baby Doll is. Hope to see you again soon." He laughed and left. What a chance meeting! Yesterday I was drunk and he was sober. Today I was sober and he was drunk.

I waited patiently, pretending to talk on the phone to make sure Bhagwan had gone. I didn't want him to follow me to the jeep and figure out I was with the police, helping them rescue Rashmi.

After a while, as I reached the jeep and sat down, Ms Sharma inquired, "What took you so long?"

"I had a call from my parents, haven't spoken to them since yesterday. They were worried. I had to take the call." I wanted to avoid telling them about my chance meeting with the pimp Bhagwan. This would have created further confusion.

Ms Sharma glared at me, but didn't say anything. All of a sudden the jeep started and we left.

"Why are we leaving? Aren't we supposed to wait for Mr Yadav?" I asked as my eyes moved from Ms Sharma to Mr Patel.

"Your work is done as of now. Mr Yadav will return to the police station on his own, and report to me. Don't leave your place and keep your mobile phone on all the time. We may need your assistance at any time," said Ms Sharma.

The police jeep dropped us at Karol Bagh metro station. We thanked Ms Sharma and Mr Patel for their immediate help.

As the police jeep left, I again looked at my mobile phone screen. Of late it had become my habit to check it every other minute. I saw that I had received a message notification on Facebook.

It was from Hazal!

37

The past catches up with Balram

"*Kanim Arkadadsim. I received gift from you today. The Siir are cok guzel. Cok Tessekur Ederim. Seni seviyorum Arkadasim J*," said Hazal in her Turkish mixed with broken English. I called it Turklish although Hazal preferred to call it Engkish.

"Where did you disappear for more than a week? I thought you had abandoned me! I am *cok sad ve angry* that you deactivated your Facebook account without even telling me!" I replied.

I set my mobile aside and decided to catch some sleep. Within a couple of minutes, my mobile buzzed with a notification.

"I am sorry *arkadasim*. I engineering college exam *ve* I couldn't concentrate. So *benim* deactivated Facebook account so I study."

I felt terribly guilty. I had branded Hazal a woman of dubious character; one who fools around with men on the internet and then disappears.

I guess everything happens for a reason. My Facebook addiction, Hazal's friendship and ultimately my misunderstanding and depression over Hazal had led me to the brothel and Rashmi. It was a blessing in disguise.

God was indeed a wizard for conjuring up perfect stories like these events. But all was not well yet. I wondered whether we would be able to save Rashmi.

"I will talk to you tomorrow, Hazal! There is lots I want to say," I typed into my messenger.

"I too lots to tell," she said.

▼

That evening I sat with Gaurav and Balram in Gaurav's room, waiting for a call from either Ms Sharma or Mr Patel. We waited, but heard nothing from them. We sat together late into the night, too anxious to sleep.

The next morning I woke up after only sleeping for four hours. Hazal's last message said that she planned to send me some gifts from Turkey and wanted my address. Surprised and pleased, I gave her my Old Rajinder Nagar address. But the truth is, my joy was overshadowed by my worry for Rashmi.

That afternoon Ms Sharma called me on my mobile phone. She asked me to come to Kashmiri Gate Police Station at 4 p.m. "Can I bring my friends with me?"

"Alright."

We reached well ahead of time and told the constable that we had come to meet Ms Sharma. He called her up and she asked me, "Didn't I ask you to come at 4 p.m.? Why have you reached so early?"

"I am sorry, Madam. We were keen to know what had happened to our dearest friend's sister, so we couldn't wait."

"We have been working day and night since yesterday to rescue her. Don't we deserve a break? Wait there patiently! It is still an hour to 4 p.m.," she said.

We waited impatiently. Ms Sharma eventually arrived with Mr Patel at 5 p.m. and they briskly went into her chamber. Soon afterwards,

Sub-Inspector Mr Yadav followed along with a lady constable escorting Rashmi and four other girls with her. The moment I saw Rashmi, I looked at Gaurav and Balram to indicate that she was Manish's sister. When she saw me, Rashmi gave a smile of relief and gratitude.

A little later, Mr Patel came out to us.

"Rashmi is a free woman now, but she has nowhere to go. We tried contacting her parents, but we hear that they are dead. No immediate relative has shown up either. We would be sending her to a rehabilitation home." I was happy and sad at the same time. This was half a victory. I wish we could take her with us then and there. But of course, that was impossible.

He continued, "Based on Rashmi's story, the police have been able to arrest two people. We are also coordinating with the Bihar Police to track down the person who offered Rashmi a job back home."

"Did the police arrest the pimp?"

"Yes, the pimp Bhagwan and also Raju, the person who picked Rashmi up from Delhi railway station."

"Can we see them?" asked Gaurav and seeing Mr Patel nod we went inside the room.

▼

The moment we entered the room, Balram gripped my hand in alarm, followed by a gentle tap on my shoulder while his eyes directed me to look at the two handcuffed men.

Raju was the same guy who had attacked Balram and me, claiming to be Shalini's boyfriend!

Raju looked at us and lowered his head again. I think he didn't recognize us. Bhagwan too looked different; the overnight custodial stay might have got him sober. He wasn't drunk and must have recognized me, but who cared! Rashmi was safe now and that's all that mattered.

Ms Sharma said, "Rashmi will be sent to a rehabilitation home for women. Keep in touch with her since you are the only person as close to a family as she has at present."

Glancing at Bhagwan and Raju, she said, "We also need her to testify against these two, so we can put them behind bars for a very long period of time."

We spent some more time at the police station talking to Rashmi and comforting her while some legal formalities were completed. Rashmi had tears in her eyes as she thanked me over and over again. I told Rashmi if it had not been for Balram, her rescue would not have been so swift and smooth.

I could see a sense of great personal satisfaction in Balram. Karma had served him well. He had not only helped rescue five girls from a terrible life, but the thought of Raju in jail was sweet indeed!

38

A Goodbye and a Gift

"Will you help me pack my stuff?" asked Balram as the three of us made our way back home from the police station in a cab. Gaurav and I stared at him.

He stared out of the window, his face expressionless.

"Where are you going?" asked Gaurav finally.

"I am vacating the room," he said.

"Why?"

"Because my father doesn't want me to stay with you guys."

"Why?" I asked.

"Because of you," he said apologetically, looking at me.

"Why? What did I do to you?"

"You have to forgive me, Alok, but that night when you guys asked me and my dad to help Rashmi, I didn't know what excuse I could give him. I thought all night through. I knew we had to save Rashmi.

"I told him you had visited the brothel and that's how you found Rashmi. I am very sorry. You know I'm a bad liar. My father would have read through the lie and wouldn't have helped us. I couldn't take the chance. After I told him the truth, he agreed to help. On one condition, that I leave the room and shift to some new room and also end my friendship with you, Alok. He doesn't want me to be friends with someone who visits the brothel."

"What you did was right. Don't be sorry, Balram. We are proud that you made this sacrifice to save a life from being ruined forever," I said, patting Balram on his shoulder.

"I will have to change my room. I have no other option, but we will always be friends. I plan to take a room nearby so that all of us can visit each other often."

Balram planned to shift to Chhattisgarh Niwas for a few days until he found another place to rent. By the time we finished packing it was close to midnight. This was his last night here. Another tenant was leaving this floor.

I would always remember the day Balram moved out… on the eve of my birthday!

What a sad birthday gift but what an epic story! Full of twists and turns; something all three of us would remember for the rest of our lives.

▼

I woke up at 11 a.m., still tired. I rushed to Balram's room to say goodbye. An empty room greeted me; he had already left! Gaurav was in the kitchen boiling water for his black coffee.

"When did Balram leave?" I asked him.

"At around 9.30."

"Were you awake when he left?"

"Yes. He woke me up before leaving. We tried waking you up too, but there was no response, even after calling you on your mobile, so he left without meeting you."

My disappointment apparent, Gaurav said, "Oh, don't make that face. He hasn't gone forever. He will be back in a week. I am sure your Turkish love will keep you busy till then."

I didn't respond and went back to my room. There were quite a few missed calls and some messages. My parents had been trying to reach me. There were quite a few notifications. Mostly birthday wishes on Facebook and SMS and WhatsApp messages. Among the crowd of messages, I saw Hazal's message on Facebook messenger. She had messaged to wish me a happy birthday, but the message had more surprise in store for me.

Hazal had sent me a birthday gift along with a letter. She said it would reach me in a fortnight. I was overjoyed with the prospect of a girl sending me a gift, and that too a foreigner!

After speaking to my parents and having lunch, I dozed off again. I woke up late that evening feeling lethargic but saw Hazal online on Facebook so started chatting with her. She sounded sad for some reason and so to cheer her up I told her about my plans of writing more poems for her.

"Please don't write many siir for me or it would be hard me to leave you."

"You don't have to leave me. We can be as we are forever," I answered.

"You won't understand *Arkadasim*. It's not easy here Turkey. Things changing and hard."

"What is not easy?"

"You soon know. I don't want you sad because of me future," she said, sounding cryptic.

"Trust me I have never been happier than this for the past three years. I have you as my friend." I never forgot to add the word friend. I wished I could directly tell her how I was beginning to fall in love with her, but I could never gather the courage to do so, fearing that she would end our friendship.

"*Tessekur ederim arkadasim*. You are good man," she said.

We chatted late into the night. Our chat was interrupted by a call from Ankit who was tense as usual. Ankit had started to sound neurotic and the way he spoke wasn't clear. Somehow I managed to end my conversation with him soon. I was worried about Hazal. I thought it was just a phase she was going through because of study pressure.

I began my work on the next set of poems for her, still hopeful that our friendship would turn into love and my poems would be able to capture her heart. In a week, as I waited eagerly for Hazal's gift to arrive, I ended up writing more poems for her. One of my favourites was:

Her Meadows

Hearing her name for the first time,
I followed, not knowing where and why,
No matter how blind I was,
She led me through her heart,
Into a meadow,
Where her footfalls still echo till today…
Hearing her voice for the first time,
I followed, with my innocence in dark,
No matter how blind I was,
She led me by the light of her eyes,
Into a meadow,
Where her smile made my heart laden with her love…
Hearing her whispers for the first time,
I followed, my first steps in love towards her,
She led me through the narrow red lanes of her lips,
Into a meadow,
Where my vacant eyes waited for her shadow…
There are a thousand ways to love that I know now,
And there are a thousand ways to kiss that I know now,
A thousand ways to kneel and hold hands in the dark,
But only one woman to feel all this for and that would be her…

I hoped with all my heart that the poems would make Hazal understand that I was looking for more than just friendship. I got four poems printed on two t-shirts, one on each side. I sprinkled them with my favourite musk perfume and parcelled them to Mersin, Turkey. I wanted my gifts to reach Hazal before her gift reached me, so this time I sent it through the costly DTDC courier. I wanted my gift to take Hazal completely by surprise, so I didn't tell her that I had mailed her the poems. I was just waiting for her reaction. My gift did reach her, much sooner than I expected.

But what followed after completely broke me down. As usual, the first thing I did in the morning, was to see what Hazal had messaged.

"*Kanim Arkadasim*. I received your *siir* yesterday. I can't tell how happy I. But *siir* also reminded me this happiness not forever. I don't want hurt you anymore ve give false hope you of friendship ve love. I love you ve I know you love me but this love no future. I hope you receive my gift soon. There is letter. It will make clear why I leave you. It was nice to know you, Alok. *Hoscakal Arkadasim*. Remember me nicely."

She had again deactivated her account, and this time, it didn't sound like she was coming back. I waited eagerly for her gift and the letter.

Finally, on 1st March, around 11 a.m., I got a call from the post office that I had received a parcel from Turkey. I had to come to the post office to collect it since I had to pay some custom tax in order to take possession. Excited, I instantly headed off to Old Rajinder Nagar Post Office.

I was surprised to see that the gift Hazal had sent was in a small square box of maybe 25cms by 25cms. I paid three hundred rupees as customs tax and immediately headed to my room with the box, carefully holding it, so as to not let it fall and destroy whatever was inside. I was never this excited even when checking out my result for UPSC.

I opened the gift, carefully removing the stamp to collect it as a souvenir from Turkey. As I removed the packing slowly, the contents of the box started revealing itself one by one. My eyes filled up with tears as I finished unpacking the gift.

39

The Letter

Kanim Alok,
Merhaba!

I asking you forgiveness right at letter beginning so you forgive me right at start of what you next read. I know I should not have extended friendship hand at first place. But I lonely ve heartbroken. I read your comments on fan page Friedrich Wilhelm Nietzsche, I went your profile on Facebook I came to know romantic poet you. I have not met you real life but you reminded me of I loved someone. That person I love now dead. I thought I would find that person in you ve decided to know you more. By talking to you ve listening to your philosophy of life and seeing you smile on Skype reminded me my lost love. Even he used to write siir for me ve when I read siir you written for me tears of joy started in my eyes flowing.

I know I very mean for me to search that person in you sitting hundreds of kilometres away. I thought it was possible. I tried teaching you Turkish thinking one day we could be together and you were eager learn Turkish but I knew things getting cok bad in ve around Turkey for Kurdish people. I hope you remember I half Zazzaki ve half

Kurdish. The regime of Recep Tayyib Erdogan not good to us nor were earlier regimes.

Peace returned starting of 2012 when there ceasefire signed between Turkish government ve PKK. I was active member PKK ve hiding for past 8 years. I joined PKK I 16 years old. My father, my brother ve many our relative's active members PKK ve they fought against Turkish authorities. The man I loved was distant cousin of mine ve was also fighter for PKK. His name Diyar Tekin. Back in 2012 unexpected happened. A ceasefire signed between PKK ve Turkish government ve government decided grant us more right ve autonomy within Turkish territory.

We celebrated thinking peace returned to our land ve we could live normal life but then in May of 2013 protest started against Erdogan government regarding freedom of press, expression, assembly, ve government's encroachment on Turkey's secularism at Istanbul's Gezi Park which spread all over country. I never wanted participate in protest but Diyar hated injustice more than anything else ve he believed secular Turkey with right to free speech would be benefit of Kurdish people ve other minorities ve so against my will ve warning he went ahead join the protest at Taksim Gezi Park to show his support for cause. He never returned.

I completely broken into pieces with loss of Diyar. There was peace after long time for Kurdish people in Turkey but this peace had no meaning left for me. I completely lost lonely ve didn't know how to recover from grief of losing Diyar. So I sought refuge on internet when I meet you felt I found someone I lost. But since our friendship began arkadasim there rise in another evil ISIS in Iraq ve Syria who has been threatening my Kurdish people in those regions. I knew that sooner or later I join the Kurdish forces fighting ISIS in Syria or Iraq. But the love, affection ve warmth you gave me only postponed the inevitable but now I leave to fight. I know by time this letter reach you I would be gone. Thanks for siir. I taking them along with me to battlefield. I would read them whenever I miss you.

I sending you Kucuk gifts. Kucuk Tavsan (Little rabbit) key chain, table clock, wind chime ve kitap on history ve struggle of Kurds. Since you called me little rabbit, I thought gifting you little rabbit key chain so that it remind you of me. Please set table clock to Turkish time so you can live in my time zone. Do hang wind chime near window. Whenever it makes sound remember girl named Hazal fighting for rights of her people.

I don't know I come back alive from this war but you keep alive me in memories my friend. Remember me nicely.

Your Kucuk Tavsan,
Hazal Demir

My eyes blurred by the time I finished reading the letter. I dabbed the letter on my shirt in an effort to dry up the tears that had soaked in. I re-read it over and over. Finally, I carefully folded the letter and put it back in the box along with the gifts Hazal had sent. I had never met this woman in real life! But the sadness I felt was more painful than any of my unsuccessful relationships.

Talking to Ankit that night didn't make things any better. For the first time in my life, I thought committing suicide may be a great option. Even listening to Ankit's perpetually anxiety-ridden thoughts and plans to commit suicide if he lost Sakshi seemed interesting. Until then, I had mocked Ankit for being weak enough to contemplate suicide. But that night, I knew where he was at because we were in the same boat. I cried myself to sleep around 5 a.m.

I never heard from Hazal again.

40

Ankit and Sakshi

I felt a heavy rock in the pit of my stomach as I lay coiled up in a foetal position on my bed. I knew I had slept way too much, close to thirteen hours! My head spun like a lucky draw wheel and I was oscillating between sleeping and being awake.

My phone was ringing. I reached for it on the table just behind the bed. I was still drunk on the idea of sleep and could barely read the caller's name on the phone's screen. I first read it as Alok. *But how could I call myself? And I had no friend by that name.* Then I reread the name and realized it was Ankit calling me.

I gave a half-dead cry, "Hello Ankit."

"The results are out and I have flunked again. I just called to say goodbye. See you and Sakshi in the next life." Ankit hung up. All I could do was say hello for a few more times, but I knew he had disconnected the call.

I jolted up from my dreamy state and sat upright in a panic. I tried calling Ankit again, but his phone was busy on another call and later was switched off. I got up to check my own result on the internet. The UPSC website wasn't loading on my laptop, so I rushed to Gaurav's room.

"Tell me your roll number?" he asked, pushing his head back on his king-size recliner seat. I rushed up to his laptop and opened the UPSC site.

We clicked on the link and waited for the PDF to download. This period was marked by silence and a smile on Gaurav's face. He knew how tense I was. When it finally fished downloading I searched for my roll number …and there it was! I had finally passed the Mains. But before I could rejoice, the next second Sakshi called me. I rushed to my room to speak to her.

"Alok, please rush to Ankit's home. He called me and was sounding weird. He has again flunked in Mains and was speaking about ending his life. Please check if he is fine or not."

"Relax, Sakshi. He must be crestfallen, so he must be saying all those things. Give him some time. He will be fine."

"Alok, please, I am very scared for him. He has switched off his phone. I have been trying to call him. He isn't taking the call. I don't have his landline or parent's number, or I would have called them up."

"I'll try calling him up. If he still doesn't take the call, I'll go to his house and let you know."

I kept on trying Ankit's phone for half an hour, but he had switched it off. Meanwhile, Sakshi grew impatient and begged me to check on Ankit.

I caught a rickshaw from Gol Chakkar. It was 7.30 p.m. I vaguely remembered where Ankit's home was. He had taken me there once, but I had waited for him at the end of the lane with Sakshi. It had been dark at that time which would make it difficult for me to recognize the house now.

He stayed in railway enclave on San Martin Marg in Chanakyapuri. I couldn't remember his house number. As the auto-rickshaw approached the main gate entrance of the railway enclave, I asked the security guard, "Bhaiya, where does Ankit stay?"

"Who Ankit, sirjee? What is his full name?"

"Ankit Gupta."

"I don't know anyone by that name, but there is one babuji whose surname is Gupta. Check out house number T-8/46."

In the glow of the streetlights, I could recognize the house. It must have been more than a year since I was last here. I wondered if his parents had heard about me from Ankit since he had never introduced me to them. There was no crowd or anything unusual that I saw, that would make me believe that Ankit may have committed suicide. *What if they don't know it yet and then I would be the one giving them the bad news!* I stopped for a second. But then I sprinted to his house, intent on making sure Ankit didn't get a chance to hurt himself.

I opened the gate and ran towards the front door. *I should not be late.* The best-case scenario would be that I was just in time to save him.

Seeing the door open I just rushed into his house. How I wish I had seen Ankit there in the hall with his parents, but all I saw were faces staring at me in surprise.

I must have looked like a madman, rushing in on them like that, but I didn't give a damn about that.

Gasping for air, I blurted, "I am Ankit's friend, Alok. Today our UPSC Mains result came out. Ankit called up saying he was ending his life because he has flunked. He isn't taking my calls, so I came rushing here. Is he all right? Where is he?"

The look on the faces turned into shock and disbelief. "How is it possible? What kind of bad joke is this?" said a middle-aged lady, probably Ankit's mother.

"Beta, are you sure Ankit called you up today?" said the old woman, who I assumed was his grandmother.

"Yes, Dadiji, he called up an hour ago. Where is he? Why don't you call him down?" I asked.

Silence prevailed over the entire room. I could see their faces turning pale in disbelief. They stared at me with wide eyes as if they'd seen something horrible.

Ankit's sister got up and went up the stairs. I thought she had gone up to call Ankit. I expected to see him come down shortly. *Phew! Thank god!*

Ankit's father walked over to me and put his hand on my shoulder.

"Beta," he said in a heavy, sombre voice. "Ankit is no more in this world. He committed suicide four years ago and today is his fourth death anniversary."

I was stunned. I slumped on the floor against a wall and felt my heartbeat slow down. "How can that be, uncle? You can ask one of our friends, Sakshi. Ankit actually called both of us."

"Did you say…Sakshi? Even Ankit used to speak about this girl, but we could never trace her. Can you please call her and let us speak to her?" Ankit's mother said, rushing over to hold my arm desperately.

"Yes, sure, aunty. I will call her on the phone right away." I said and dialled Sakshi's number. To my absolute dismay, all I could hear was the operator's pre-recorded message, "This number does not exist."

I tried the same number over and over again. I had spoken to Sakshi so often on this number, but the same message greeted me, "This number does not exist."

From my expression, they understood that Sakshi's number was not reachable.

"Is 9565896574 Sakshi's number?" asked Ankit's father, looking into his mobile phone.

I looked into my phone to cross-check the number. "Yes, uncle, it is!" I said. My brain was numb! *I just spoke to Ankit! How are these people saying he died four years ago? Are they even his parents? Is someone playing a prank on me? Did I come into the wrong house!? What the hell is happening!!*

Ankit's father guided me to a chair and made me sit. Right opposite the chair on the shelf I now spotted Ankit's picture with a garland. Quite a few incense sticks were burning as if some puja had just been conducted. It was the Ankit I knew!!

Ankit's father said, "We got this number from Ankit's mobile four years ago in March 2010, when he committed suicide. He was going through a major depressive phase. He was an IAS aspirant. It was his third attempt and he couldn't take it anymore. We even took him to a psychiatrist, but it didn't work out. The psychiatrist said that Ankit was showing signs of schizophrenia because he was under immense pressure. Ankit had himself told us about Sakshi and how he planned to marry her, but we could never trace the girl before or after his suicide. We wanted to know what exactly made him take such a drastic step over an exam in which failure is so common."

I was speechless.

"Did you clear the Mains, by the way, beta?" asked Ankit's father, when he noticed that I was staring at Ankit's picture.

All I could do was nod.

"All the very best, beta. I don't know how you managed to get in touch with my dead son, but if you do meet or speak to him again, do tell him we miss him a lot," he said with a deep, anguished sob. That triggered off his mother and grandmother too.

I left without saying a word, still shaken and not yet able to come to terms with the sudden turn of events. *Whose voice had I heard almost two hours ago on the phone? Who was Sakshi?*

In the days leading up to my interview, which was almost two months from now, I remained mentally disturbed.

I tried sharing my burden with Gaurav, but he managed to come up with a scientific explanation for the story I told him.

"You were under tremendous pressure to clear this exam. Maybe that's why you started seeing a person. In medical terms, it is called schizophrenia. Tell me why you don't see Ankit and Sakshi now and why you no longer receive their phone calls? Because now you have cleared Mains and the pressure has eased.

"I have a friend who is studying MD in psychiatry at AIIMS. Just meet him. I will arrange for the meeting. A few medicines and consultations and you will be fine again."

"Why don't you understand, Gaurav? You also know Ankit used to visit my room."

"If he did as you are saying, why haven't I ever seen or met him? I don't recall seeing any person with the physical description you have given me about him," said Gaurav.

I asked Rohini, Indu, Balram and everyone else, they all said the same thing. They had never met Ankit or Sakshi in real life and had only heard about them from me.

I tried tracing the identity of Sakshi, but it led nowhere. I went to all the coaching centres we studied at, but they were not able to retrieve her admission form. They only kept the admission forms of the people who had cleared and the rest were disposed of. *Who was Sakshi Singh Chauhan? Would she always remain a mystery?*

At my UPSC interview, one of the panel members had asked me to narrate a story, given that I had stated that writing stories was one of my hobbies. So this was the odd tale I narrated.

Little did I know that on 26 May 2014, on the very fateful day of my interview, Sakshi's story would also unfold for me.

41

After the Interview

When at last I walked out of the interview room, I was certain that the interview had gone on for very long, almost an hour.

Now, standing in front of me was one of the panellists, who had told me something that shocked me out of my composure.

"Son, I am Ex-IPS officer Rudrapratap Singh Chauhan. The girl you mentioned in your story – everything you said about her, every personal detail, it matched with my daughter's. Did you really know her and meet her in real life?" he said. I cannot describe the expression on his face. There was a shock, sorrow and wariness... and under it all, there was hope.

A shiver ran down my spine. He was talking about Sakshi! The girl whose voice I had last heard two months ago on my mobile phone, begging me to help Ankit.

"She committed suicide in August of 2007 while she was preparing for UPSC because of our opposition to her marrying some guy from some other caste. We never thought that she would take her life as she was always an obedient girl. We had no idea she kept her real emotions hidden from us. In her suicide note, she blamed us and the pressure of studying for UPSC as the reason for her suicide." Sakshi's father's voice was jerky, trembling with emotion. He pulled out a photo from his wallet and showed it to me. "Was this the girl you were talking about?"

I nodded. It was indeed Sakshi. He then put the picture back in his wallet, pulled out his visiting card and offered it to me. "Keep it. Get in touch whenever you feel like after the results are declared. I would like to talk to you in detail about how you met my dead daughter and what she confided in you."

He walked back to the interview chamber. My mind in a whirl, I stood staring at his retreating back, completely and utterly out of my depth.

▼

The roads in and around Chanakyapuri, India Gate, President House and Parliament were blocked for security reasons because on the very day of my interview, Shri Narendra Modi was going to be sworn in as the new Prime Minister of India. I made my way home from Dholpur House tired, after being stuck in traffic for an hour, with my head filled with more questions than I had ever handled. I was disappointed since my interview had not gone as planned. But the mystery over the real identity of Sakshi was finally solved.

I sat in my room connecting the dots, putting the pieces of the puzzle together.

▼

I knew the ghosts of Ankit and Sakshi had been with me during my journey of studying for the UPSC exams. I realized they meant no harm to me. They only wanted their story to be told. They knew I was a writer. Who better to pick, after all?

They wanted the world to know how their lives were sacrificed at the altar of parental and societal expectations. I was the medium they had chosen for their story to be told. Through me they wanted the world to know about it.

Even I was on the verge of breakdown and surrender, but god had other plans for me. How I wish Sakshi and Ankit had survived their hardships and tribulations, but I guess their destiny was already written. Perhaps because of them, I survived the gruelling time I was preparing for the exam. Ankit became the person who provided me with an outlet for my frustrations by voicing them for me.

Epilogue

The result of my interview was out within a fortnight. I had made it into the list, though barely! I looked at the ring on my finger and the gemstone in it reminded me of the prophecy of the astrologer. Later when the scorecard of the selected candidates was released, I discovered that I scored heavily in Mains, especially in the newly introduced paper of Ethics and Integrity, but managed only 120 marks in the interview.

I couldn't complain. I was more than happy to see my name in the list considered sacred by many. I met Sakshi's father and after telling him the whole story all over again, all he could do was blame himself for the suicide of his only daughter.

Balram and Rohini too made it into the list that year and with an even better rank than mine. When the service allocation list was declared, Balram was allotted IPS while Rohini made it into IRS (IT). I was going to become an IAS albeit in instalments! I made it into DANICS!

Gaurav decided to join DNB Surgery in Government Medical College, Kolkata. Indu had cleared State Bank of India Probationary Officer exam and was working in Hyderabad.

The journey of becoming an IAS only made me realize what a struggle life is and how uncertain it is. It reminded me of the short lives of Manish Pandey and Abhijeet Singh. Rashmi's story reeked of human greed and how it made greedy predators force fellow humans into sexual slavery, just for money. Mustafa's story was all about the extent to which one can go for love, which often leads to disappointment, belying the hype. God only knows what happened to Hazal!

The story of Ankit and Sakshi, so familiar and rampant, was the story of too many bright young sparks; sparks which were smothered under the weight of society's unreasonable restrictions.

▼

Ten lakh aspirants think of writing the UPSC exam, seven lakh fill the form, six lakh write the exams, and only a thousand or less get selected. I was one of them.

This is my story – the story of Alok Shirke.

But my friends, the story of the rest of my life is yet to come. I don't know where and when it will end. For now, as I speak, I am on my way to Guwahati to meet Mr Das and young Bulbul.